FLOODED SECRETS

THE CHRONICLES OF NEREZIA - 2

FLOODED SECRETS

Published by The Kraken Collective
krakencollectivebooks.com

Edited by Dove Cooper.
Cover by Eva I.
Character Portraits by Vanessa Isotton.
Interior Design by Claudie Arseneault.

claudiearseneault.com

ISBN: 978-1-7389259-2-6

THE CHRONICLES OF NEREZIA

AWAKENINGS

FLOODED SECRETS

THE SEA SPIRIT FESTIVAL

STORIES FROM THE DEEP
(Coming January 2025)

MOTES OF INSPIRATION
(Coming April 2025)

RUINED HISTORY
(Coming 2025)

LOST TRADITIONS
(Coming 2026)

TANGLED PAST
(Coming 2026)

UNDYING LOYALTY
(Coming 2026)

FLOODED SECRETS

THE CHRONICLES OF NEREZIA - 2

Claudie Arseneault

Kraken
Collective

This book is written in Canadian English. If you are unfamiliar with it, it may appear to "switch" between American English and British English spellings. Those are not mistakes; the words are spelled as intended. Thank you!

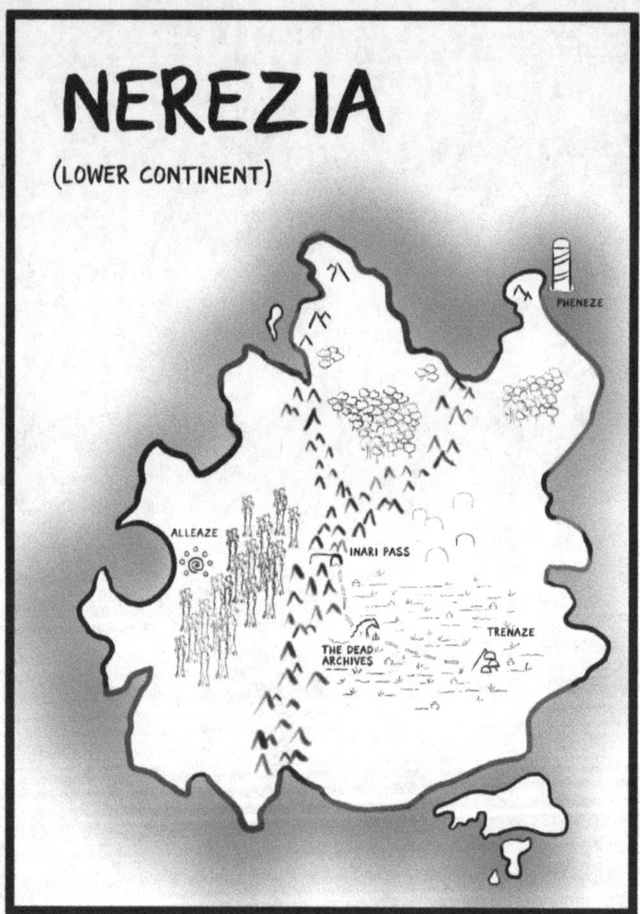

NEREZIA
(LOWER CONTINENT)
PHENEZE
ALLEAZE
INARI PASS
TRENAZE
THE DEAD
ARCHIVES

Horace (e/em), Embo Extraordinaire

Excitable and talkative, Horace has taken half-formed skills from eir many failed apprenticeships to become the Wagon's main cook.

Aliyah (they/them), Mysterious Stranger

Left with the strange ability to transform into an eldritch tree and the memory of a mystical forest, the quiet and perceptive Aliyah is on a quest for answers.

Rumi (he/him), Anxious Artificer

Rumi travels the world in a magical Wagon and springs his marvelous creations on the isolated cities of Nerezia. He disguises protectiveness and anxiety under pessimism and grumpiness.

Keza Nesmit (she/her), Thorny Protector

Confident and abrasive, Keza is a thorny companion who knows her worth. Under the spikes hides fierce and loyal love.

So far in
The Chronicles of Nerezia

Horace's trial day as a guard for eir home city of Trenaze should have been simple: stand watch, guide locals to the correct stalls, meet the incredible artificer who travelled into town in a magic wagon, and guard the giant glyph that maintains the city's protective dome.

Simple… until a mysterious person in a porcelain mask slips past the glyph's protection and deactivates the dome, allowing the glowing shards that haunt the outside world, possessing people or slicing them to pieces, to dive down inside, fusing together in a single, monstrous amalgam of Fragments.

Armed with a sword, a shield, and far too little training, Horace rushes to defend the market-goers. But eir last stand is interrupted by a mysterious elven figure who can dissipate the Fragments with a single, strange sentence: your story is my story.

From the moment it is uttered, Horace knows the sentences holds true for em, too—and when the elf collapses in the middle of the market, e carries them to safety, to recover away from the panicked crowd and inevitable questions.

This stranger, Aliyah, has but one desire: to leave Trenaze's safe boundaries and find the forest that haunts their dreams. After an afternoon of board games in their quiet, sharp-witted company, Horace is ready to follow. They leave with Rumi, an anxious artificer and travelling salesman, in his Wandering Wagon of Wondrous Wares, a semi-sentient self-propelling wagon which always remains safe from Fragments.

Life on the road isn't quite the adventure Horace expected, but e keeps emself busy by cleaning and cooking—and when e finds a popular card game, e gathers eir newfound companions for a few rounds, further cementing the bonds uniting them.

They eventually reach the Dead Archives, a waypoint reputed to be safe from Fragments and the home of beautiful crystalline formations. Horace's exploration of the Dead Archives is interrupted when e runs into the stranger in the porcelain mask again.

The encounter is brief and brutal, leaving

Horace on the ground, dagger at eir neck, as the self-proclaimed Archivist demands that e leave Aliyah's side and return home. They call Aliyah the Hero and are convinced they can awaken Fragments, and although Horace doesn't understand what that could mean, e knows one thing: eir place is at Aliyah's side, no matter the danger. So e refuses to leave.

Danger comes calling immediately: Aliyah's scream echoes down the Dead Archives' corridor, followed by the sound of a fight.

Horace rushes to eir friend's side. Fragments have possessed dead bodies and have surrounded them, pleading for release in rattling voices. And every time one touches Aliyah, they buckle as the corpse sighs in relief and collapses.

Horace does eir best to extract eir friend, shielding them against the Fragments with eir body, but the sheer number threatens to overwhelm them both—until Rumi comes to the rescue.

With the help of an engineered force field, Rumi pushes back the bodies, and Horace runs out with an unconscious Aliyah in eir arms. They scramble into the Wagon and leave the Dead Archives.

It takes Aliyah days to recover, after which they admit that they may pose more of a danger than anticipated, and that they remember nothing before Trenaze, except the cursed forest in their dreams, which they hope is home, and full of answers for them. Horace mentions the Archivist's belief that Aliyah can awaken the Fragments, and together they decide to assume none of the Waypoints will be safe.

Rumi knows which forest Aliyah seeks, but it is on another continent. They plan a route that would take them through the nearby Tesrima Ridge using the Inari Mountain Pass, and from there, to the coastal city of Alleaze.

And so the story continues…

The ripples of our inciting incident were certainly unexpected, but we chose to let them run their course. The Hero chose Their companions, and Their companions chose Them—who are we to interfere? We will monitor them all closely, with special care to the untrained guard, so that eir weakness does not portend everyone's doom. But I have hope. For the first time, I have hope for our broken world, and confidence that my departure from traditions was a necessary sacrifice. History will not judge me harshly for it.

Archivist Neomi

1

The Dangers of the Road

Horace trained every day.

Weeks ago, a mysterious and lethal Archivist in a white grinning mask had predicted eir eventual death, and the subsequent events had only proven their point. E was ill-equipped to defend anyone—not emself, and certainly not Aliyah, who seemed destined to attract danger. Since cleverness had never been eir strong suit, e had opted to train eir muscles and fighting skills.

Travelling in a magical Wagon didn't offer em the most practical space, but Horace managed as best as e could. Every morning e climbed to the Wagon's top platform while the vehicle rolled on, moving of its own volition, and e went through a routine of push-ups, sit-ups, and any other exercise e could remember from eir brief stint as an apprentice for Clan Zestra, eir desert home's guards. In the afternoon, e ran circles around the Wagon. E was careful not to go too far; staying close to the Wagon was all that kept em safe from the Fragments roaming the landscape around them. The glimmering shards bled golden light and reflected the sun at Horace as e trained, their eagerness to possess a victim doused by a sustained avoidance of the Wagon itself.

Over the weeks of travel, the ground grew rougher and steeper, injecting some variety in eir daily run. They'd crossed the red sand desert to journey northward along the Tesrima Ridge, following the road up and down its slopes and making headway towards the Inari Pass. According to Rumi, lush forests and a striking blue ocean awaited on the other side of the stony peaks, along with the seaside city of Alleaze, where they could book passage across the water, and from there travel to the forest in Aliyah's dreams. Once the road veered deeper into the mountains, Rumi assured them the Pass was less than a day away.

Their path sometimes overlooked steep cliffs, giving Horace vertigo if e looked over the

Wagon's side, or passed right under them, creating walls of stone that blocked the sky unless e craned eir neck. When either happened, Horace let the training slide and allowed the beauty of the world to sink in.

Eir home city of Trenaze had been gorgeous, in its own way. It had perched along a single craggy mountain, spread across its two plateaus and the flat ground at its foot, each section protected from Fragments by a large, pinkish dome. For the longest time, that pink had tinged the colour of the sky, and even now Horace still startled at the sheer *blueness* that unfurled over eir head. The world, for all its dangers, was full of wonders, and e wanted to see them all.

Unfortunately, e got to experience the dangers first.

They were rolling under a particularly steep cliff, the Wagon creaking its way along the narrow path. Aliyah was sitting on the platform, repairing tears in their cloak while watching Horace train. E had been holding a front stance, following a pattern of exercises Trenaze's guards had shown em, stretching eir muscles and counting seconds before switching to another position, when a shadow flickered at the corner of eir vision—a flash of burned orange dropping down. It landed in front of Horace, and e registered the thick fur of a felnexi before a wooden staff hit em—one, two, three; hip, arm, back of the knee. Pain flared through eir body and e staggered backward with a wheeze, eir sight blurring from tears.

Aliyah jumped to their feet with an alarmed gasp, and their attacker spun on themselves in a single fluid motion, a high kick striking Aliyah's chest and sending them flying off the platform. It happened so fast, Horace only registered it as e heard the gut-wrenching scraping of Aliyah hitting the rocky ground below.

Fear bubbled through Horace and e dashed for the side of the Wagon that Aliyah had tumbled over, ignoring their assailant entirely. Which might not have been the brightest move. The felnexi stepped in eir path, grabbed eir wrist, and—despite Horace's bigger gait and weight— they pulled em forward, slid under em, then used Horace's momentum to roll em off their back and slam em on the platform. Air rushed out of eir lungs, and eir whole body seized in protest. Dimly, e realized the Wagon had stopped rolling.

The felnexi leaned above em, sharp teeth showing from their wry smirk. "You got interesting priorities, big fella."

They had a strange rolling accent, almost like a purr. Horace didn't have enough air to answer, could only gasp as they tapped eir forehead with the staff mockingly and leaped off the top of the Wagon. Horace dizzily contemplated the orange tail that'd vanished for a few seconds before e realized they'd gone straight to Aliyah. E crawled back up on eir knees and found the attacker with their clawed feet right at Aliyah's throat.

Curse all the glyphs, e was supposed to be getting stronger to prevent exactly this.

"What in the blighted Fragments is—" Rumi's high-pitched voice cut short as he emerged from the Wagon below. Sunlight gleamed on his blue scales, and his rows of sharp teeth snapped shut as he took in the scene. "Oh no no no, these roads are *deserted*! What now?"

The felnexi laughed at that. "Do I seem like the desert to you? I know the colour's confusing, but I'm not calling you the sky 'cause you're some shade of blue." They leaned forward, and Aliyah squirmed under them as the tip of their claws prickled their skin. "Now, I'm sure travellers with a fancy wagon like yours have got some food to spare, hm?"

Food? They were doing all this for a meal? Horace pushed emself fully up and gripped the railing. "Oh! You could have just asked! There's no need for all this, we'd be happy to share."

Below em, Rumi grumbled in what sounded awfully like a protest. But why would he? They did have plenty of food to go around. Except maybe there was something Horace didn't understand, because eir offer brought another sharp laugh out of the felnexi.

"No, I mean, *all* of it. And quick! I don't have all day. The roads are full of poor innocents to steal from!"

Now Horace knew they were pulling eir legs, because they had been travelling for weeks and this strange felnexi was the first person they'd met.

"You can't take all our food!" Horace said. "What would we eat?"

"Not *my* problem," they replied. "Now get to it."

Rumi huffed and stomped back into the Wagon, grumbling every step of the way. Horace's gaze flicked between Aliyah and the roof's trapdoor opening. E should help—with Rumi's three feet of height, he'd have a hard time dragging anything out—but e didn't want to leave Aliyah alone with this felnexi. Aliyah themself didn't seem nervous, though. They'd brought a knee up and slid a hand under their head, making themself comfortable, so Horace buried eir misgivings and went inside.

Rumi greeted em with a loud, "Can you believe this asshole? All our food!"

He'd found an empty crate and was placing cans of pickled vegetables into it, his tail tracing his anger in quick twitches. Horace leaned over the much smaller isixi and retrieved the strips of beef jerky that had impressed em so much upon eir first investigation of the Wagon cupboards.

"So much for all the hours I spent

reorganizing the kitchen."

It'd been a way for Horace to put eir home out of eir mind and to figure out what exciting new ingredients e had to cook with, but it'd taken em several days to sort through a mess they were now giving away.

"Never mind your cleaning! This is gonna ruin me." Rumi waggled a tiny finger at Horace, his voice dropping. "Whatever you do, don't say a peep about the reserves. We need *some* food to survive."

Horace pouted. Sure, e had a big mouth and it ran faster than eir brain, but e didn't want to starve, either. "I'm not gonna tell them anything."

They filled two more crates like this. Horace piled them up, then grabbed the bottom one and ambled towards the exit, blinking against the sunlight as e reemerged outside. Neither their assailant nor Aliyah had moved, so Horace set everything down halfway between the Wagon and the felnexi.

"Here you go," Rumi declared. "Emptied the whole cupboard."

The attacker's tail flicked and their ears flattened. "I doubt that's all you had. You're on the road for a long ass time, aren't you? I bet you have one of those fancy cold boxes."

"So what?" Rumi's shoulders hunched and he hissed in the first real display of aggressivity Horace had ever seen from him. "What are you even doing here? Who *are* you? None of this makes sense! There isn't a settlement for miles around, so how do you survive?"

"Questions, questions, questions." They wagged their entire tail with every word, their calm a mockery of Rumi's twitching anger. "I can give you a name to curse. Keza Nesmit, she and her, at your service."

She threw her arms out, and the shift in weight made her clawed foot dig in deeper in Aliyah's chest. Horace stepped forward, but before e could say or do anything, Aliyah raised a hand and stopped em.

"She's not alone."

Aliyah declared it with such conviction that Horace glanced up at the cliff above, expecting felnexi to swarm them from everywhere.

Nothing.

"I advise you accept what has been offered and move on, however," Aliyah continued, a dangerous edge creeping into their voice. "Remove your foot now."

Horace's gaze flicked back down. Aliyah had grabbed Keza's ankle, their finger thickening into a bark-like skin, lengthening and wrapping around it. A soft pale green glow shone through the fabric of their clothes, heralding more. Since when could they control the roots? Whenever Horace had seen Aliyah transform, it had been into a full tree-like being, and they'd not seemed themself.

Keza looked down, and her eyes widened. "Fuck the stars."

She tore her ankle away, bringing her staff at the ready as she leaped off Aliyah. Little burgeons had erupted at the tip of her weapon that had been on the ground, and the sight dragged another curse out of her. Aliyah sat up calmly, and most of their transformation seemed to recede. Horace studied them for signs of the usual exhaustion that followed any tree-like shapeshifting, but if they had any, they hid it well.

"I'd rather not," Aliyah said as they rose. They turned towards Horace and Rumi, nodding solemnly at each. Their motions did look a little stiff now. "Let's leave the crates and keep moving."

The Wagon creaked half an inch forward in response. Horace's gaze bounced between Aliyah and Keza, then from Keza to the crates, and finally towards Rumi. E hadn't stepped away yet, and now that this stranger didn't have claws ready to tear through Aliyah's chest, maybe e could…

Keza must have followed eir reasoning, because her tail fluffed up with aggression and her ears flattened. "I'll kick your ass again if you don't haul it in the Wagon and leave my food alone."

She didn't need to prove that she could. Horace's muscles ached from the first brutal fight. "Right. Let's go, Rumi."

Rumi clearly didn't want to go, but he was the smallest of them. He clacked his teeth once, in warning.

"Good luck with the booby trap," he said, before scampering back into the Wagon.

"What booby—" Horace stopped emself, catching up to the lie.

Too late. Keza was already laughing.

"Nice try, shortscales."

A frustrated cry emerged from the Wagon in answer. Horace's cheeks burned. E'd ruined that one, with eir loud mouth and slow wits. Well. Not much to do about it now, and the Wagon was starting off again, wheels crunching the rocky road.

"All right then," e said. "Gotta go, so, huh… Have a nice day of banditry?"

Keza saluted in return, and the moment e backed off from the crates, she stalked closer, placing herself between Horace and the precious food. E couldn't quench eir reluctance at abandoning it all, no matter how casual Aliyah seemed about it. Even just looking at it made eir stomach grumble.

"Best get going, big fella," Keza said, gesturing at the ever-more distant Wagon.

She was right. E didn't want to get left behind.

With a quick jog, Horace reached the Wagon and climbed on the back, holding onto the frame as e cast one last glance at the felnexi, leaning lazily on her staff as she watched em with burning orange eyes.

"Years of travelling, and that must be the rudest, most awful experience I've ever had."

Rumi was stalking circles in the Wagon, tail swishing with angry energy, claws scraping on the wooden planks. He had been doing so for the full half-hour since they had left Keza behind and didn't seem inclined to stop anytime soon. Sometimes the Wagon punctuated Rumi's rants with a clack of the door, or the heavy curtain to Rumi's workspace getting pulled or drawn suddenly. That, too, was new. It hadn't done anything like it in their first weeks together.

"I wonder if she does that often," Horace said. "She was pretty skilled."

Maybe that was why she'd had *Nes* at the start

of her name. In Trenaze, that was the particle to denote masters in a vocation. The rest of her name hadn't been any clan e knew of, though, and they were far from Horace's home city.

"I don't care how skilled she was!" Rumi threw his arms up. "She was awful, and she stole all our food."

"Not all of it," Horace pointed out.

"Why are you defending her?"

"I'm not!" Horace lifted eir hands, palms out, before Rumi jumped em. He had grown so twitchy with anger! "It's just ... we still got a little, right?"

Or so e hoped, anyway. None of them had inventoried what was left, and they had put quite a lot in those three crates.

Rumi harrumphed. "Yeah, yeah. A little. Not enough to make it to Alleaze, but the road on the other side of the Ridge passes through a giant forest. I know there's a guide somewhere about edible stuff, so we can probably gather as we go."

He hopped over to an enormous trunk, as high as he was tall, and climbed into it. The inside was full of books of all sorts, some old and dusty, others slim and in a well-preserved leather binding. Rumi rummaged through them, discarding almost everything he picked up, muttering throughout the entire search about rude felnexi and being forced to scavenge for food and how he had better things to do and hoped they were both ready to contribute, since they'd been so eager to give Keza those crates.

Laughter started to bubble through Horace at the sight—Rumi, perched halfway in a trunk, throwing books about as he ranted to himself. Eir gaze met Aliyah's, and once e saw eir own amusement reflected in theirs, e couldn't contain it any longer. E snickered, then Aliyah coughed over a chuckle, and suddenly they were both laughing, eir booming voice covering their softer one. Rumi stopped his search to stare at them.

"What's so funny?"

"Nothing," Horace said, out of breath—because nothing *was*, really, but with the stress of the brief and brutal encounter evaporating, *everything* was, too. With a contended sigh, e repeated, "Nothing, I swear."

"Not sure I believe that," Rumi mumbled. "Did she knock your head too hard?"

Horace grinned. "Maybe she did? But we're alive and moving towards the Pass and none of us are going to starve, so I could just think it's better to laugh at it than let it ruin the day. It *was* pretty impressive. You should have seen her."

If Horace could fight like that, e would be a lot less worried about protecting Aliyah. Perhaps given enough time, e'd get to a semblance of that level. Although if e was honest, e doubted e'd ever develop the fluid agility Keza Nesmit had displayed. Even half of it combined to eir raw strength would go a long way, though.

"Maybe you're right," Rumi conceded. "But it'll make it a lot harder to purchase passage in Alleaze's harbours. If I could just find—ah!"

He brandished a thick tome, then climbed out of the trunk. Rumi had to stretch on his tiptoes to close the top, but once it slammed down with a sharp *thwack*, he turned back to Horace and Aliyah and tapped the cover of the book with renewed enthusiasm.

"With this, we can manage. I hope you're both

up for a lot of forest exploration once we're on the other side of the Pass. No more bandits, only mushrooms. Easy-peasy!"

It all sounded perfectly reasonable until they reached Inari Pass.

2

Flooded Pass

"Maybe we're cursed," Rumi said, staring at the road where it dipped into black waters and vanished from sight.

It had been a full day since Keza Nesmit had dropped on them from above, kicked Horace's ass, and demanded most of their provisions, but their luck had only become worse since. They'd discovered that the cold box had broken overnight, and although Rumi had fixed the glyphs up front quickly, the fish inside had unfrozen enough to need immediate attention—and that was almost half of their proteins.

Then the clouds overhead had solidified into rain—actual rain!—and it flooded the road and forced them to stop on higher and safer ground.

No deluge could dampen Horace's enthusiasm, and e had spent a good chunk of the night with a lantern out, withstanding the rain battering eir head and soaking eir curls as e marvelled at the water skipping and churning along the rocky path, careening downhill. When e'd returned, Rumi had blasted em with one of his hot-air gadgets, loudly declaring e would drench everything inside otherwise.

Intent on still making the best of the situation, Horace had proposed a few games of *Proteins*. That, however, had led to the discovery of two missing city cards, perhaps misplaced when they'd last played after a meal, and thus later slid by accident into the three crates stolen from them. Regardless, a thorough investigation of the Wagon didn't unearth them, and Rumi called it quits and decided to go to bed.

"Tomorrow we'll go through the Pass, and all these bad memories will be left behind."

The Inari Pass, as it turned out, was completely flooded.

"I don't understand," Horace said. "How did all the water even get here?"

The Pass wasn't, as Horace had first expected, a narrow valley between two peaks. It was a high underground passage that snaked from one side of the mountain to another, and in some sections the walls sported carvings with beautiful curve patterns reminiscent of ancient dwarven art, along which a luminescent green moss grew. They felt like guides, accompanying travellers down the path. Horace had been so absorbed by them, e hadn't noticed the water until the Wagon had lurched to a stop.

It lapped at their collective feet now, and the tunnel plunged into it, the green moss glow becoming fuzzy with depth and distance. Despite the gentle slope, the water eventually reached the ceiling and would drown the Wagon if they kept rolling forward.

"A curse," Rumi reiterated, clacking his teeth. "Why else woul this Pass, used for centuries, would be flooded the day we necd it. It's rained before, and I never heard of anything like this."

"I do not think it is rain," Aliyah said, and their soft whisper echoed in the tunnels. They edged closer to the water with a concerned frown, and Horace wondered what *else* they thought it could be.

Rumi started pacing, tail swishing, and Horace caught a few words of his mutterings—something about underwater breathers, and waterproofing the Wagon.

"Can't you just … drain it?" Horace asked him. "Like a, huh … pump, is that it?"

"And send it where?"

Horace shrugged and gestured vaguely behind them, only to realize the road sloped downward and the water would return. E hadn't thought that one through. Maybe the incline crested soon, and they could still do it? It seemed easier than everything Rumi had mumbled about.

"This is not rainwater," Aliyah repeated, more firmly. They had dipped their hand in it—and all around their fingers a slight yellow glow pulsed, there and gone for a moment. Aliyah's brow furrowed with concentration. "It is also draining out, albeit very slowly, but more pours in on top of it. The passage will flood further. If we could get to the source, however, we could stop the flow and, in time, lower the water level."

They straightened up and looked at the ceiling, as if they could trace the water stream through the rocks.

"I know where the source's at."

When Keza Nesmit's voice bounced through the tunnel, all three of them froze. Horace spun, muscles tense and ready for a fight e'd inevitably lose, but the felnexi didn't jump at them. She was perched on top of the Wagon, clawed feet gripping the edge, staff lazily set on her knees. Horace half-expected the Wagon to buckle and try to shake her off, but it stayed still, surprisingly silent about her presence.

"When I say we're cursed..." Rumi began, before gesturing at Keza. "What do you want this time? Have you been following us?"

"Oh, yes, absolutely. Stalking your every step from the shadows, ready to jump you." Her voice dropped into a low, dangerous purr as she answered, and she slid off the Wagon to approach Rumi. He quickly backed away, only to find the water lapping at his scaled feet. Once she'd trapped him, she leaned down with a predatory grin. "You'll never be rid of me."

Rumi hissed, and his tail slapped the water behind him while his eyes darted from side to side, looking for a way to escape. Horace doubted he'd be fast enough, if Keza didn't let him. E stepped closer, just in case the threat was more serious than e thought.

"I'm confused," e said. "Where did you leave the food we gave you?"

Keza laughed heartily and leaned back—and in that split second, Rumi scampered around her to slink behind Horace's tall legs, staying just far enough that he could pretend not to be hiding with some dignity.

"I ate it all," she answered.

"She is lying," Aliyah said. "The food must have been brought back to those she stole it for in the first place."

Keza's mirth diminished, and although she tried to maintain the relaxed, no-care attitude, Horace noted the tension in her shoulders.

"*Maybe.* Y'all make the lies too fun and easy."

Aliyah's eyebrows rose, and they acknowledged the rebuttal with a slight nod.

"Then allow me to speak the truth as I understand it, since it seems so hard."

Their dark eyes settled on Keza, who returned the stare, and it felt as though energy gathered between the two, a contest of wills that Horace and Rumi could only spectate. When Keza found her words, her voice had turned tight and sharp.

"Go ahead."

"We had no choice but to come here, so you did not need to follow us. You brought the crates back to your community, then headed straight for the Pass. You must have known it would be flooded, and I suspect the cause of it is tied to the cause of your stealing."

Keza's face didn't move, but her tail swished with nervous energy. She kept her silence, orange eyes still on Aliyah, evaluating them with more seriousness Horace than had seen from her yet. She was saved from an honest reply by an outburst from Rumi.

"Oh, I get it now. Whatever's causing this is ruining your life, too, so you figured 'Hey, maybe those fools I brutally robbed yesterday won't hold it against me and can go fix my shit.

After all, they need to get through. They either succeed and I don't have a problem anymore, or they die and I steal what's left. Win-Win."

Keza leaned on her staff, and a purr-like rumble emerged from her throat as she grinned. "Right on, shortscales. So … you up for it?"

"No!" Rumi threw his arms up. "We're not helping *you*."

"But Rumi," Horace started, "how do we get through otherwise?"

"I'll build something, anything. I totally can! There's *always* a solution in here."

He tapped the side of his head. Horace suspected there were fewer solutions than petty revenge in it at the moment, because Rumi had forgotten one very important thing.

"Can you build it in a day? Two, at the most?" Horace asked. "We're in a bit of a hurry. No food, and all that foraging is on the other side."

The choked gargle coming from Keza sounded dangerously like a laugh. Rumi glared at Horace, and the cavern echoed with the horrifying noise of his small, sharp teeth grinding against one another. It lasted so long

Horace thought he'd snap one. Then Rumi stomped once, releasing the frustration.

"I can't," he admitted.

"I would have gone anyway," Aliyah said softly. "There are Fragments in the water. We do not want to test the Wagon's ability to withstand a flood of them."

Horace didn't relish the idea of plunging the entire Wagon in Fragment-filled waters either, with or without Rumi's wondrous inventions. Fragments might have avoided it while travelling, but what would they do if the Wagon was forced upon them like that? Strike back? Try to invade to possess the occupants? Not to mention they had a bad habit of acting up around Aliyah, growing stranger and more aggressive in their attempts to reach them. E turned towards Aliyah.

"Are you sure it's safe for you to be near the water?"

Their lips flattened and they breathed in deeply, no doubts chasing memories of their dangerous encounter at the Dead Archives before returning a smile to em. "I will be counting on your support. We can do this."

Warmth spread through Horace at Aliyah's confidence in em. Despite the training of the last weeks, e hadn't exactly felt up to the task and Keza's quick assault hadn't helped. But if Aliyah thought e could do it, who was e to refuse? With a nod, e turned to the remaining member of their little group.

"Yours too, Rumi," e said. "We wouldn't have made it out without you last time."

"And yet here you are, throwing yourself at more problems despite my advice." For all his complaining, Rumi walked back to the Wagon and patted the side of it. "Sorry, buddy, I guess we're turning back and taking on an unwanted passenger. You'll let her in, right? Cause I won't hold it against you if you don't."

Keza tilted her head, lips pursed in a confused expression. "Talking to the Wagon?"

"Indeed," Aliyah replied, "and I advise you afford it a decent amount of respect. I would not want to find out what it does to intruders."

Keza's ears flattened with actual fear. "Right. I don't think it can come where we're going, but

I suppose we can stick with it until then."

Rumi snorted at that, turned around, and met Keza's gaze with a grin. "This is the last time you underestimate the Wagon, you furred fool."

Rumi's confidence in his Wagon was entirely warranted. Keza led them back out of the Pass, then down a fork that had been concealed by a large rocky outcropping. At first the Wagon only rolled through, but the road quickly became a trail of massive boulders and steep climbs. Keza hopped on the tallest rock, and once she had a plunging view of the Wagon, she called out.

"How are ya gonna roll through all this?"

Horace thought she had a point: even on foot, this path would be a struggle. But Rumi only laughed and climbed down, then out.

"We're not rolling, of course."

He touched the wheels of the Wagon, and runes lit up along them, spokes and frame turning a beautiful teal. Then the wheel itself cracked, splitting into long wooden arcs with reinforced steel inside. The Wagon creaked and lifted, lurching forward in the motion—and in the span of one wonderful instant, it had transformed from thick wheels to high, flexible legs with adjustable length. Horace whistled, all other words gone from eir mind.

"And it's not gonna slide?" Keza asked, but she couldn't muster any conviction to her doubts.

"Nope. It's got grip." Rumi ran scaled fingers alongside the curved legs, his tail moving in low, prideful swings behind him. "It's the first modification we ever worked on together, and it has never failed me."

He climbed back up, using old spokes as bits of ladder, then went through the inside to join Horace and Aliyah on the roof. His grin widened at their impressed faces.

"Hold on," he said. "The ride's bumpier this way."

The Wagon lurched forward again, rocking back and forth with each long stride. Its legs adjusted to some extent, but between the changing heights of the boulders and the natural movement of the walk, they shifted about a lot. Boxes and tools slid around inside, crashing to the ground. Maybe that accounted for some of the mess Horace had initially found in the Wagon, though after weeks of living with the scatterbrained isixi, e knew Rumi had the lion's share of responsibility.

Keza spent most of her time guiding them on the path, springing from one rock to another. They hiked along the mountainside, slightly upward without ever leaving the valley in which the Inari Pass' tunnel entrance had been located. Horace stayed atop the Wagon, gripping the railing in case their ride bucked and threatened to throw em off, and eir gaze swept the desert below.

E had never been so high, not even at the top of Trenaze's Nazrima Peak, and the rocky red soil of eir homeland unfolded far under them. Bushes and trees dotted the desert, sometimes closing ranks into a serpentine strand of green where a rare brook ran. It was denser than the few spots of vegetation around Trenaze, and more beautiful for its contrast with the barren surroundings. Irregular stone formations rose in jutting spurts—some in thick flat cylinders, like short dwarven fingers, while others spread in wide mesas. No matter how hard e peered at the horizon, however, e could not catch a glimpse of the single-peak mountain where Trenaze thrived. They had long since left home behind, its three pink domes little more than a memory e held dear. Still, e wondered what upheavals had shaken the city after e'd fled with Aliyah before they could interrogate them about the dome's failure. Had they tracked em to Varena's establishment? If so, how did Varena fare and was she angry at eir departure—or at em stealing the saira boards?

"Homesick?" Aliyah's presence surprised em, and despite the softness of their voice, Horace's soul burned with the accuracy of the question.

"A little. A big little."

They nodded with a noncommittal sound, setting their dark gaze on the horizon. Could Aliyah know homesickness when they had no home to speak of? Was the compulsion from their forest dreams laced with a similar, quiet nostalgia? Aliyah placed their hand on eirs, and then it felt like it didn't matter whether they truly understood or not. Horace smiled at the gentle touch and let it fill the silence between them—a moment of comfort in the absence of words.

In time, though, eir gaze drifted back to Keza, tracing their path through the mountain, and to the incoming task.

"What do you expect will happen once we're there?" e asked. "What do you think we can *do*?"

"I do not know. There were Fragments in the water—small bits, almost more echoes of them than the actual shards. As it seems my mere presence is impacting them, I am hoping it will be sufficient to trigger events we can handle."

Right. Not the most reassuring of answers, was it? But it was honest, at least. E grinned and puffed eir chest out. "We'll deal with it when it happens, and then even Keza will be impressed with us!"

Eir voice carried farther than intended, bouncing off the rocky mountainside, making Keza pause and turn around, tail swishing in what felt like mockery. She stared in their direction for a split second, then sprinted to them with a burst of speed that morphed her into an orange blur. She landed next to Horace before e'd even registered what was up.

"Trying to impress, big fella?" she asked, leaning casually on the railing, her body swinging along the Wagon's movements with grace.

"Yeah," e blurted out, honesty taking over any semblance of reserve. "I mean—"

Keza's laugh interrupted em, saving em from having to say anything else. She slapped eir shoulder. "I like you. Horace, right?"

"Yes. Horace ka-Zestra, e and em." None of them had ever introduced themselves, had they? Not that they'd had much of an opportunity the first time, but since it seemed they'd be together a while longer... Names helped. E tried not to think of eirs, and how e'd abandoned eir Clan and should not claim it anymore. "And this is Aliyah, they/them. Oh, and there's Rumi, of course. He/him."

"The Wagon got a name and pronouns, too? Cause y'all act like it's a whole person."

That was a good point, wasn't it? They'd all grown used of thinking of the Wagon as having some degree of sentience, but Horace had never bothered with further questions.

"It *is* Rumi's Wandering Wagon of Wonderful Wares. So I guess that's its name?" Horace shrugged. "Rumi just calls it Wagon, so I always figured that had to be it."

Keza tapped her claws on the railing. "It's very fancy."

"You can't steal it." Horace blushed as the protective warning escaped em. If she meant to hijack it, telling her not to do so wouldn't change anything.

Keza grinned at em. "Can't I?"

The Wagon lurched in protest, throwing them all off balance, which brought a barking laugh out of her, the sound sharp and honest. She leaned on the railing with a low purr, and the Wagon settled into a more tranquil pace, and Horace couldn't help a panicked glance at the steep incline they were travelling against. A fall would break their bones. Then again, Horace had a feeling they were all about to attempt something much more dangerous.

3

The Source

Keza led them to another opening into the mountain.

They did have to leave the Wagon behind this time: for all of its magic, Rumi had to admit it could not, in fact, diminish its size and it definitely did *not* fit through the entrance. He made a big fuss about it, warning Keza that if she had any friends hiding and waiting to steal it, they'd all pay for their audacity. Horace, having shared this very fear and given it far too much thought, didn't see how one would force the Wagon to move if it didn't want to.

Unlike the Inari Pass, which had the winding feel of a natural cavern repurposed and decorated, this entrance had been carved with tools. The same glowing patterns were etched into the walls, sweeping curves of moss that provided some meagre light. At times, the green was joined by a soft blue from flowers that climbed as vines, even on the stone. Cool humidity filled the air as the group ventured deeper, and the faint echo of trickling water reached their ears. It grew as they progressed until they turned a corner and it became a clear rush.

The sound came from a larger rectangular room with a sweeping arched ceiling and a myriad of fancy waterways. Water arrived from multiple holes in and near the ceiling, pouring into canals that converged towards a great, bulb-like structure in the centre. The bulb itself resembled a giant glass orb encased in stone and overran with the same glowing moss as the corridors. It ended in a solid base on the floor, and in the dim light Horace could trace a number of stairs going to the base, or rising from it, to reach higher parts of the bulb.

These led to a second set of canals, from which water would exit the bulb, guiding it back into walls or along other existing tunnels. Horace counted five, each with its own small pool and access platform, each at different heights of the bulb.

Water wasn't pouring out from any of them. Instead, it gushed out of a large crack in the bulb, a third of the way up, and splashed on the ground before following grooves into the floors. Those guided the solid, steady stream into a side opening that dipped downward.

"That overflow is how your pass got flooded." Keza gestured to the water with her staff, before pointing it up, towards the lowest canal out of the bulb, almost at ground level. "But that's where the problem is."

Aliyah had already started in that direction, but Horace was still absorbing the room as whole—the majestic bulb, the shimmer of the glowing moss in the water, the peaceful gurgle of streams, the intricate patterns carved in the stone. People had lived here, built this, left their mark inside the mountains. E squinted suspiciously at Keza.

"Do you know what this all is?"

She shrugged. "Waterways. And a problem."

She knew more, didn't she? She had to, if

she'd brought them to this place. Considering how she purposefully turned her back on em to hop towards the suspect canal, however, she had no intention of offering more. Horace huffed and followed.

To eir surprise, water *had* gathered in the tank outside the lowest of the bulb's openings, an extra storage space large enough for four people. The small pond at its bottom had nothing in common with the clear streams abovehead, the ones that rushed *into* the bulb. It was a shifting mass of sharp golden shards and viscous mud, most of which tightly congregated near the grate that led into the tank. Glowing flecks danced through the inch of water that must have made it past.

"Those are Fragments all right," Rumi said.

So a writhing heap of Fragments was blocking the water from exiting the bulb. E craned eir neck, looking once again at the crack farther up where it all gushed out instead. If they opened the way below ... wouldn't the water level lower, and it'd stop leaking?

Aliyah walked to the golden mass, paying

little heed to the beautiful construction and mossy designs, and stared at the water, eyes slightly unfocused, head tilted to the side as if listening in. Horace edged closer. E didn't trust this whole 'Fragments blocking the water' thing. Fragments didn't do that. They roamed around and stalked people, and cut their way into them to take over. Why these ignored the four nice targets was beyond em, but with Aliyah this close…

"And this clogged canal usually leads somewhere useful to you and yours, does it not, Keza?" they asked.

The question earned them a silent glare. They stared at each other for long seconds, and the twitch of Keza's tail grew increasingly aggressive.

"Perhaps," she admitted.

Horace turned to her. "I don't understand why you're so secretive! We're all here to help and we already gave you all this food. I'd love to learn more—about them, or you."

Rumi's whine of doubt made Horace whirl around, eir jaw dropping. E knew he and Keza didn't exactly get along, but Rumi didn't need to make it that obvious. That was so mean.

"Why don't we all focus on the task," Keza said. "This problem happens once a year, but I've always been able to unclog it. This time it reformed in my face."

"Must have been *soo* frustrating," Rumi piped up. "Kind of like you showing up when we thought we were free."

Keza spun with a dangerous grin, casually unhooking her staff. Rumi's tail twitched and he hopped back, even though she didn't feel threatening, in Horace's opinion.

"Let me give you a little demonstration."

She climbed down into the small reservoir, and her fur raised as she touched the muddy water. Tension lined her shoulders, but she began a slow sequence of strikes with the staff, the motions fluid and powerful, almost a dance in their own right. At first nothing happened, and Horace watched for the beauty of it. Then the water inched away from a swish of her staff, a tiny jerk that became a wave with the following strike until every sweep pushed the layer at the bottom farther. Keza moved closer, spinning and dancing, and directed her next attack towards the Fragments.

They scattered with the first slice, mud flying against the bulb and leaving yellow shards behind. Keza's stance widened, intense concentration furrowing her brow as she strode forward and chained another sweep, the force of her technique breaking chunks off of the murky Fragment block. Water slid through the cracks she pierced, pooling at her feet in the temporary tank, then trickling into the canal and beyond. The quiet stream turned into a gush as she kept working, freeing the waterways. In a matter of seconds, the water level had made it to her knees. The Fragments that had been blocking it hovered above, long and jagged, spinning very slowly on themselves. Horace held eir breath, convinced they'd dive for Keza at any moment. She ignored them, looking back up at the group.

"Usually that's all I gotta do. They wander away, and it's a done deal. I'm good until next year."

As if on cue, the Fragments' spinning sped,

and the horrible grinding of metal filled Horace's ears. E shouted a warning as the shards swooped down, and the golden glow mixed with the water, turning into a viscous substance. One by one, the shards slammed at the bottom of the basin, at the opening leading into the canals. Yellow light sloughed off the Fragments and into the pool like a strange glowing ooze, a single muddied pile clogging it up. Keza leaped out and stared at both, her ears flattened.

"Great. Now they don't even let the tank's water flow. I didn't need it to get worse."

"I'm afraid they will never abandon this task," Aliyah said.

"Look, I don't give two shits if they wanna waste their eternity on this, but I need them to go back to trying this whole drainage control once a year and easily leaving. They got real stubborn this year for some reason."

Aliyah grimaced, guilt flickering through their expression. Were they blaming themselves for the change? But the Wagon had only just arrived in the neighbourhood. Then again, they'd only just gotten to the Dead Archives when something had called to them inside.

"Well, I bet we can be even more stubborn!" Horace declared, projecting confidence e didn't have. Everyone had grown too serious and e didn't like it. "All we need is a plan."

Aliyah lowered themself and extended an arm out, reaching as close to the fast-rising water level and Fragments within as they could. Horace's heart leaped in eir throat, but none of the Fragments reacted. No jumping at them, no grinding, metallic shriek, even. So much for that idea.

"Rumi," they said, "do you remember the force field you created at the Waypoint? Could you make two of those as spheres, to protect most of the tank from the Fragments? Keep them away from the exits?"

Rumi's lack of enthusiasm preluded his answer. "That field would've blocked water, and it's not built to last unless I leave the rods behind."

Aliyah's eyebrows raised in a challenge. "Are you not able to modify that prototype into another closer to what we require?"

That didn't sound simple to Horace, but the

change in Rumi was instantaneous. He squared his little shoulders and tipped his head up with pride. "Of course I can. My wares *are* wondrous, after all!"

"How long do you need?"

Rumi's gaze settled on Keza and his tail gave a defiant swish. "You'll have it next morning, and it'll take care of it more permanently than some fancy magic battle technique."

Horace had seen Rumi tinker. In fact, e'd seen Rumi tinker almost every hour of their travel days, and many of the nights, too. He'd stand at his workbench, bending and twisting metal bands, sawing and sanding and carving wood, fitting gears together and testing his machinery. Sometimes he talked to the Wagon, a one-sided conversation with their partially sentient locomotion.

E'd seen Rumi tinker, but e'd never seen Rumi *work*.

Gone was the casual play with parts, the mindless woodwork as he worked through problems in his mind, the sudden *"oh wait!"* of inspiration, or even the *harrumph* as a device collapsed into its parts. Rumi's happy tinker sounds were replaced by a string of mutterings, only punctuated with long, serious thoughtful humming. He moved with precision, reaching with the pincers and wires he needed without lifting a dozen different ones first, and the goggles often over his head almost never left his eyes now. It was as if all of Rumi's explosive energy had been resorbed into his small body, then transformed into pure focus.

Horace left him to the grind, setting a plate of flatbread and hummus spread at the edge of the workshop table, then climbed on the Wagon's top platform. Keza perched on its railing, holding tight with one hand and both clawed feet. How could she be comfortable like that, crouched on a thin rail? Another mystery, as far as Horace was concerned. E elected to lean in a corner while Aliyah sat by eir side.

Perhaps comfort wasn't why Keza chose that

seat. She hadn't touched her food yet, and her eyes remained trained on the mountainside, as if they could pierce through it.

"Your secret people you won't talk about … do they know you're here?" Horace asked. "I'd be terrified, in their stead, if someone didn't come home by night. You can't just sleep outside with Fragments all over the place."

Keza's gaze flicked to em and moonlight caught in her eyes, reflecting it. "Wouldn't you *love* to know, eh?"

"I would!"

E didn't understand why she was so adamant about these secrets. And of course e wanted to know! Why wouldn't e?

She laughed, and her tail swished before wrapping around the railing. Horace expected her to fall silent and provide no answers, but instead she conceded, "They'll worry. But this is worth it."

"A temporary ill for a permanent solution," Aliyah put in.

Keza replied with a low, purr-like sound, then finally began eating. Horace tried to get more conversation out of her a few times, but she refused to talk about her community, or how she'd learned to move water and Fragments with her martial technique, or even whether or not her second name was related to the Trenaze's *nes* particle to denote masters. That one just seemed to confuse her.

E eventually gave up on the personal and retrieved the saira boards. "Let's see if you can learn this as fast as Aliyah did."

Keza snorted, looking first at the wooden board, then at the colourful dice. "Really? Children's games?"

Horace's eyebrows shot up. Why would saira be for children? What a strange thing to say. "I play it. That makes it an adult game, no?"

E held eir breath. In Trenaze, *adults* had completed an apprenticeship and been adopted into a clan. E had fled before Clan Zestra could reject em and add one too many failures to eir record. To people there, e was an eternal child despite being far older than the average age for induction into a clan.

"Put that way." Keza slunk down from her perch and crouched opposite of em. "We got time to kill anyway, so why not? Teach me your adult ways."

Horace let the hint of mockery in her tone go, too relieved not to be called out on eir adult status. Besides, she'd see once they started playing! Nothing childish about the multitudes of strategies one could adopt in saira. E went over the rules of choosing dice from the pool, placing them on the board, and combining them to create special effects—and after a while, Keza only stared at em, eyes narrowed but blank, as e continued.

"You're supposed to remember all that?" she interrupted halfway through the combos. "That's bullshit."

"Children have excellent memory," Aliyah said, earning a confused look from Horace. Did they? E'd grown up with saira and had never considered the patterns could be a lot to learn; Aliyah themselves had had no problem. "I can help your first few games."

Her ears twitched and flattened. "No way. I can handle myself."

A first game demonstrated the lie there—or, well, perhaps that was unfair. Keza *could* handle herself, in so far as she very confidently broke every rule she couldn't remember. Horace protested at first, which led them into stare downs over the boards—and Keza proved *very* good at those. When she kept going, Horace threw a few desperate and overwhelmed looks at Aliyah, who was doing their best not to laugh. With the speed at which e was losing the game— assuming they'd count points as normal, anyway—e needed a new strategy.

If Keza didn't care for the rules, then neither would e.

Horace began inventing combos, declaring very loudly that placing a cross of yellow dice allowed em to exchange eir own with Keza's, or that e was shielded from the next steal when the proper pattern for this power was far from eir reach. E lacked Keza's deadpan attitude for bluffs, however, stumbling over eir half-truths or overexplaining the parts that were false. Aliyah's raised eyebrows confirmed eir clumsiness, but Keza didn't seem to notice until the fourth and most egregious lie. She tilted her head to the side, one ear twitching, and met Horace's gaze. Eir cheeks burned, betraying em.

Keza burst out laughing—a frank and predatory sound that sent eir heart spinning. Her tail swept forward, wrapping under her crossed legs, and she tapped the platform with a claw.

"Now we're playing," she said.

From that point on, the only untouchable rule became that Aliyah had final say in whether an invented combo should be allowed or not. Most of them were, but Keza and Horace got too daring a few times and Aliyah slowed their game-breaking bluffs into something more reasonable. They invented moves with the dice pool available, wits and daring working double time—or so it felt to Horace, whose entire head throbbed from thinking so hard and fast. Without eir knowledge of existing combos to serve as inspiration, e wouldn't have kept up with Keza. She lied with bright confidence, moving dice about as if she'd played this game all her life. By the time their boards were full of dice, hers exhibited far higher values than eirs … and made a triangular cat face with two ears to boot. She grinned at him.

"See? I can handle myself."

"That was *exhausting*," Horace said, flinging emself against the railing behind.

"But fun," Keza countered.

"But fun," e admitted.

Aliyah leaned forward, dragged Horace's saira board closer to them, and picked up the dice, returning them to the bag as they cleared the board. Calm certitude imbued every movement, captivating Keza and Horace, who watched in sudden silence. Once Aliyah had finished, they set the board in front of them and looked at Keza.

"Now it is my turn." They pushed away the torn cloak that tended to envelop their lower body with casual and fascinating gravitas. It was as if a dark flame burned within Aliyah's eyes, dragging one's attention and commanding respect. They smiled—a slight raise of the lip, perfectly poised. "Where I am from, there are stakes to any contest. Losers owe others a story. Any story. Are you game?"

A low rumble emerged from deep within Keza's belly. "You're all stubborn little priers, aren't you? But I can't decline a challenge."

She swept her board up and upended it, scattering the dice around. Horace helped scoop them up, focusing on the task at hand to avoid throwing confused looks at Aliyah. Where they came from? But they didn't remember any of that, did they? Were they … oh. *Oh.* They just wanted Keza's story! If they could lie like that… E grinned, eager for the match.

They played the game in a much calmer fashion than the speedy combo creation contest Horace had held with Keza. Aliyah paused before their dice picks, and the lies rolled off their tongue with such ease that Horace caught emself mentally reviewing the rules. Even more impressive was the lore Aliyah built around each combo, describing the origin of its name or legendary players that had used it, weaving an entire world with the seriousness and comfort of one instructing a newcomer to the most important tenets of their belief. They spoke of mighty ramparts against an invading enemy, of large ships lifted into the sky by crystal magic, of masked carnivals and poisoned drinks and unbearable catastrophe, and before long Horace and Keza paid more attention to their tales than to the game—so much that when Aliyah placed their final die, they both startled, as if drawn out of a trance.

"How in the cursed stars did that happen?" Keza asked, her voice softer than Horace had ever heard it.

E had to admit, e wasn't sure either. Eir mind moved slowly, emerging from the fog of beautiful stories it had nestled in. Aliyah only shrugged.

"I think I won."

Keza burst out laughing, and the energetic noise dispelled the rest of the molasses around Horace's head. E shook eir whole body, sounding somewhat like a horse in the process.

"Don't believe I can tell any stories like you do," Keza said. She hopped to her feet and stretched out, long and slow. "But I'll think of one. Promise."

She did not give it to them that evening, instead slipping back down into the Wagon. As Aliyah didn't protest, Horace contained eir disappointment. The two of them stayed up under the night sky for a while longer, their gazes lost into the sprinkled stars above. Silence blanketed them, warm and comfortable, sliding off them only once Horace asked about the wondrous worlds Aliyah had painted earlier, and where they drew their inspiration.

"These are the things I dream of when the grove does not occupy my nights," Aliyah said.

"It's beautiful, I think."

"Me too."

Aliyah was more than happy to add new details to their previous tales, slowly building an entire universe for em while they huddled on the Wagon's roof, their silence at times punctuated by the clinks of Rumi tinkering below.

4

Explosive Solutions

Rumi's solution was an explosive device no bigger than his fist, made of a small crystal encased in long wooden braces, every inch of which had been inscribed with glyphs. The crystal itself emitted a soft glow that changed colour, and when Horace bent over the sphere to get a better look, e felt its power—a tingle running across eir skin, a low buzz at the back of eir mind. Rumi had been very adamant that the force field would balloon outward and could be dangerous if it was too close to them. How he could say that then hold the bomb like it was no big deal was beyond em.

Then again, Rumi himself was more jittery

and twitchier than usual. His tail swished and tapped a lot, and every now and then he'd lose track of his words and stare in the distance, only to blink hard, clack his teeth, and return to the present. He refused to let them handle the tiny bomb, bringing it close to his chest when Keza joked about yanking it from his hands.

"No one's foolish enough to let *you* play with anything that explodes."

Keza cackled, and for most of the walk back towards the giant reservoir, she made half-hearted swipes at Rumi. She only stopped once Horace stepped between them, using eir thick body as a shield against even Keza's speed. She took it as a signal the game was over instead of as a challenge, and returned to her position slightly ahead of them, scout and guide.

The bulb's room was as they'd left it, except for the very obvious overflow from the open basin where they'd been yesterday. During the night, the water level had risen to the brim, and it'd spilled over and down, following the grooves in the floor towards the walls, and into the same hole that'd go on to flood the Inari Pass below.

Horace grabbed eir sword and shield as they climbed the few steps to the lowest grate and its adjacent tank. If Aliyah's proximity was what had stirred them into stubbornness despite their recent arrival, what would they be like after another day?

Rumi stopped at the edge of the basin, staring at the water still overflowing onto their platform, then down to the ground. "So, huh … hate to say it, but this is way deeper than I'm tall. I can't jump in." He tapped the surface with the tip of his tail. "You mind clearing it out?"

He didn't turn towards Keza as he asked, but who else could that have been meant for? She laughed, bonked the top of his head with her staff, and hopped into the water. "Sure thing, shortscales."

Warm joy spread through Horace's chest at the prospect of witnessing the dance again. This whole 'let's make the Fragments clogging the place explode outward and block their return' plan made em very nervous, but if it meant a chance to watch Keza another time? To see her slowly impact the flow of water with her sweeps? E'd take that risk.

She had more water to contend with this time, and started her dance on the reservoir's lip, building her rhythm before dipping the staff through the surface. Water swirled around it, clinging to it as it emerged then flew overboard. Horace studied her carefully as she emptied part of the basin, trying to decipher the flow of her stance changes, parries, and attacks for a key to its supernatural effects. Except for all eir good intention, e lost emself in the dance again, eir mind serene as eir eyes and body tracked the elegant motions, the way water sometimes attached to the staff, sometimes flitted away from it, as entranced as e was.

Then Keza started a constant spin and leaped into the tank, staying close to one side. Water fled her path, rising in a whirlpool around her, the glowing yellow mud clinging to the walls. The writhing pile of Fragments blocking the water flow shone brighter, right at the edge of her cleared circle.

Rumi tapped Horace's legs, drawing em out

of eir trance, and signalled for help getting down. Horace lifted him, a hand under each shoulder, then lowered him into the tank, first by kneeling at the rim, then by flattening emself to go as low as e could before dropping Rumi, whose shoulders hunched as if he expected the water to crash on him.

Rumi crawled towards the mass of Fragments one tiny nervous step at a time. His claws grinded on the wooden contours of his bomb from the tightness of his grip. Against the backdrop of viscous yellow silt, the jagged edges of the Fragments, and the menacing glow of the blockade, he seemed small, insignificant. His tail flailed behind him, the rapid swings betraying his fear as he stretched and set the device down into the Fragments' mud. Rumi scrambled back with a yelp as soon as it clicked, one arm raised as if he'd expected the shards to come flying at him, and everything from his shoulders to his tail drooped in relief when it didn't.

"Let's get out of there," Rumi squeaked, hurrying back towards Keza.

"How long do we—?"

The device cut her off with a high-pitched whirr and a harsh blue glare. Keza swore loudly as the light grew even brighter, and the last thing Horace saw was her leaping forward, towards Rumi.

Then the miniature bomb exploded.

Blinded, Horace stepped in front of Aliyah with eir shield raised, blinking furiously to chase the aftereffect of the flash. A brutal shockwave slammed into eir shield, splattering it with slimy mud and water. E slid backward, ears ringing, and held eir balance only through sheer strength and good reflexes. When Horace's vision finally cleared, e scrambled back to the rim of the basin, terrified for eir friends.

Keza stood at the bottom of the tank, her staff spinning in an endless and desperate circle above her head. The movement kept the water at bay, forcing it to flow all around her as it rushed for the newly formed hole. Rumi was at the edge of this cleared circle, fallen down, his tail bent in what must have been a painful angle. He ignored it, staring at the result of his work.

A shimmering blue dome had replaced the

pile of Fragments and mud clogging the exit, latching to the opening and sealing it tight, creating a shield for everything within two feet of it. A dozen Fragment shards floated above, some big and menacing, others small but no less deadly. They rotated with terrifying speed, as if propelled by their anger. Two slammed into the shield, sparking bright light with each assault, but the defence held. Like Trenaze's dome, but blue instead of pink. Horace's chest clenched with remembered fear as another pair smacked into the blue barrier, only to be pushed back.

Rumi instead threw a small fist up with a cheer. "I did it!"

The Fragments froze at the sound of his voice.

They hovered, and the low buzz slowly morphed into the screeching of steel on steel. Horace thought eir ears would start to bleed from the sheer intensity of it, and Rumi whimpered, clamping hands over his ears and curling up.

The Fragments took it as an invitation. They flew at him, the screeching intensifying and harmonizing all at once, and Horace's heart sank all the way to eir heels. E could never leap down and get to Rumi in time to protect him.

Keza swore again, so loud it covered the Fragments' screeching, and stepped forward, sweeping her staff in a horizontal arc. She knocked a first Fragment of course, then spun and smacked a second into the tank's wall. A quick change of grip brought her weapon around, and she hit two more—*thwack and thwack*—as Horace stared, open-mouthed. She never stopped moving, fighting off water and Fragments both, a deadly whirlwind all around Rumi while he crawled and pressed himself against the wall, desperate to evade the onslaught—all until a single Fragment slipped past her, its jagged body surfing on a recursing wave before it sank into the side of Rumi's body. A choked yelp of pain escaped him, and he turned to stare at the foot-long shard now embedded into him.

"Oh."

Small claws touched the glowing Fragment, and a golden mist drifted from the shard to glide over Rumi's arm with hungry eagerness. For a moment, Rumi leaned towards it, the terror washed away from his face. The first specks of mist slid between his scale, slipping into his body. The Fragments' solid shard cracked, turning into a thick golden glow that clung to Rumi's wound. Panic surged within Horace. Was that how they possessed? Were they losing Rumi?

Keza landed from a spin, her staff flying right through the haze, pulling it along as though it was a sticky web. Rumi jerked and gasped, then his eyes rolled back and he collapsed.

"Get him out of there," Aliyah said, voice sharp with command.

It drew Horace out of eir daze, and e scrambled down into the water. Keza had lost control of the pool through her fight, and it sloshed back over Rumi, threatening to drown him. The Fragments still danced about her, and as Horace picked eir little inventor friend up, e couldn't help but notice they were slowing. It felt, unexplainably, as if they'd all perked up, waiting.

Then e sensed it too, in the air all around—a buildup of power, like the steady and inexorable rise of water. E tightened eir grip to Rumi, who was dripping blood and water.

"Aliyah?" e asked.

"I feel it."

"Some real bullshit's coming our way," Keza said, her voice dropping into a growl.

Water clung to her ankles, but since the Fragments had stopped flying her way, she lowered her staff. She panted heavily, and her tail drifted in slow, tired motions on the surface. Horace placed Rumi at the edge of the pool, then heaved emself out. Eir own breath felt difficult, as if the very air had grown thick and stale. No … not stale, e thought. *Charged.*

A low rumble echoed through the cavern, as if answering eir thought. It shook eir bones and heart. Something *was* coming. E scooped Rumi back up, holding him protectively.

Aliyah gasped and fell to their knees, one hand reaching for their chest. Horace whipped towards them, and they met eir gaze, deep dark eyes seeking reassurance. Under their fingers and clothes, a soft green light began to glow.

"Aliyah…"

"I can't—I can't control—"

Panic scrambled their usually calm voice, and it spread to Horace immediately. E knelt at their side, grasping their shoulder with eir free hand.

"I'm here. I'll be here."

To do what, e had no idea. But it had to count, right?

With a resounding crack, Aliyah's body shifted. Bark crawled over their skin as their limbs lengthened, popping with every new knot in the wood, every branching twig. Their back hunched, their face transformed into sharp edges of wood in which two pale-green eyes glowed fiercely. They looked up, towards the great bulb-like reservoir.

"Everyone with me," they said, voice now deep and scratchy with power. "Away from the tank. *Now!*"

Aliyah moved down the stairs, growing branches slamming into the stony steps, carrying their body a few inches above the ground. Horace scrambled after em, eir grip tight on Rumi as they relocated to a more open space.

Aliyah stopped there, their chin tilted up, pale green light leaking from their eyes. Keza leaped out of the tank, water splashing after her, and sprinted after them. Horace barely saw her move—one moment she'd been in the water, the next she'd slipped behind Aliyah, staff at the ready. Every inch of her fur was raised, and her ears were flattened as she waited, poised. The pressure in the room increased until it became almost unbearable.

A soft sound emerged from Aliyah—wind rustling through leaves, the delicate snap of twigs, the groan of heavy wood, all merged with one another in a strange melody as they lifted a hand, fingers transformed into twisted branches. Their body burgeoned, slim offshoots spreading from palm and chest and legs, cracking as they extended into a sphere around them, hundreds of tiny twigs linking up together. Horace's mouth had gone dry and e tightened eir grip on Rumi as the wooden dome grew. Keza let out an almost plaintive growl.

The Fragments once clogging the tank circled nearby, thin slices of golden light through the branches, their metallic screech a counterpoint to Aliyah's forest melody.

"Come, friends," Aliyah said in that strange, eldritch-tree voice.

The air *whooshed*, a great wind sweeping into the room from the many arched openings, and light built in them. Yellow light—the golden glow of gathered Fragments, ever closer. Horace stiffened, heart hammering, feet rooted to the ground as surely as if e, too, had transformed into a terrifying tree. The harsh glare grew blinding, but e squinted against it, determined to see the friends Aliyah had called.

Hundreds of shards flew in, a flock of Fragments melding into a gigantic snake-like amalgam. Its great maw opened, rushing for them. Horace brought Rumi closer, shield raised in a desperate—heroic and pointless—attempt to protect the others if it pierced through. E braced emself for the impact … and it never came.

The second of stillness that followed seemed to last forever. Horace was acutely aware of the roughness of Aliyah's bark skin against eir own, of the weight of Rumi in eir arms and the wetness of water and blood in eir shirt, of the low growl from Keza beside em. The air smelled of thunderstorms, mould, and blood.

The snake—a thousand jagged shards constantly rearranging themselves into the gigantic beast—slowly filled the room, wrapping itself around and over their small sphere, as if to constrict it. It brought the outside basin's water with it, swishing through its golden body. Horace watched with horror. What could they do against such a creature? Could Aliyah truly hold it at bay, and for how long? Rumi was bleeding, and there couldn't be that much blood to lose in such a small body.

"This shit's thicker than a pea soup," Keza said, her voice tight. She was right. The Fragments had grown so numerous e couldn't see through the cloud anymore. "Was *that* the plan?"

Horace offered a confused shrug in response. They hadn't really had a plan, had they? Aliyah and Rumi acted like they'd figured it all out, so Horace hadn't worried about it. E'd trusted they'd had the strategizing covered. Now that they were trapped under a giant amalgam of Fragments, however… E glanced at Aliyah, their limbs long and twisted from the transformation, more unreadable now than ever.

"It'll be fine," e added, and the certainty in eir voice echoed to em, more profound than e'd anticipated. Grounded by it, e fought eir swirling terror and repeated. "It'll be fine."

The snake lowered its head, pressing its nose against the top of the dome. Horace half-expected it to collapse under the weight, leaving them all at the creature's mercy. What would that feel like if dozens of Fragments tried to possess em all at once? Would they tear em apart from the inside, erasing all traces of whom e'd been? Would the pain shut em down immediately? What *did* it feel like, to lose one's self into the Fragments? E'd heard the stories of people condemned to cycle through the same movements over and over, reenacting a single moment until they collapsed from exhaustion, but no one had ever escaped it to tell the tale.

Aliyah pressed their palms against their dome and it retracted with gentle pops, allowing their hands through until they settled crooked fingers on the two flat slits of the snake's nose.

"Your story is my story," they said, and the scratchy voice had an undertone of rustling leaves, softening it into a nostalgic tone.

Horace held eir breath. E'd heard this before, in Trenaze's Grand Market, when e'd met Aliyah. Fragments had pierced the city's shield and fused together into a beast, attacking them. That was when e'd first witnessed this strange tree form of Aliyah's—and they'd touched a Fragment with similar gentleness then, too, reciting those words.

"Your pain is my pain," Aliyah continued, spreading their fingers. "Your joy is my joy. Your life is my life."

The Fragments stopped moving, stopped rearranging themselves along the snake's long body. They froze, the constant grind of screeching of metal vanishing. Horace knew what came next, and e couldn't help but mouth it along with Aliyah, a pledge of eir own.

"Your story is *my* story," they concluded.

Their shield of twigs crumpled to dust,

punctuating Aliyah's words. They didn't flinch, didn't even seem to notice; their entire focus remained on the great snake.

It began dissipating. The golden mist vanished first, disappearing from the area near Aliyah's palm, but even the jagged shards vaporized. The effect spread, spiralling all around them as it followed the length of the snake's body, gaining speed with every circle. For a time, only a yellow mist remained and water glittered with its light, sparkling with an ephemeral beauty no one else would ever witness. The sight burned itself into Horace's mind, precious and unique.

Then the haze swirled—a single spin, as if winding itself up—and rushed towards Aliyah's open palm. Water splashed the entire group as the mist sank into their hand. Aliyah's body braced, absorbing it, one leg sprouting multiple roots to hold them steady. Along their arm, however, the bark began to recede, and Horace knew what this meant. E dropped eir shield and, keeping only Rumi, e wrapped eir thick arm around Aliyah, catching them long before the roots vanished and their legs gave in.

Silence returned to the cavern, broken only by the gurgle of water running along the carved canals and into the bulb. The basin no longer overflowed, instead draining out from the grate now protected by Rumi's blue dome.

Keza stared at Horace, her wet fur clinging to her wiry body. Her eyes caught the glow of the moss along the walls, reflecting it in an eerie way as she scanned the room.

"That all sure happened," she said at last. "They dead?"

The question dropped rocks at the bottom of Horace's stomach. Aliyah wasn't, e knew that much from experience, but e quickly set both of eir friends down to get a better look at Rumi. Blood drenched his clothes and scales, and his tail curled up around him in a pathetic attempt to protect him. Horace brought eir cheek close to Rumi's mouth, and a huge wave of relief spread through em as e felt the tiniest of breaths.

"N-no," e said. "But Rumi's not—I can tend basic wounds, but all the blood…"

"Forget it."

Horace's head snapped up and e glared at Keza. Forget it? E wasn't going to just give up on Rumi like that! "How can you say that? He helped you. He's dying because he helped you!"

Keza growled and dropped her staff. "I don't have time for this. Neither does he. Step back."

What? Horace only responded with a confused stare, but Keza had already moved on. She tore part of her sleeve off and shoved it as best as she could in Rumi's wound, then picked him up.

"Keep my staff safe."

And she sprinted away, through the passage opposite of the one leading to the Wagon, a blur of orange against the moss's green glow, vanishing before Horace could protest. E stared long after Keza had gone, eir mind filled only with the sound of water behind em. Finally, at a loss of what else to do, Horace picked up Keza's staff, swept Aliyah in eir arms, and trudged back to the Wagon.

5

Keza's Secret

The Wagon did not like Rumi's absence.

It creaked and groaned at Horace, slamming cupboards e'd barely touched and pulling the heavy curtain that closed off Rumi's workshop from the rest of the interior. Horace had never been this self-conscious within its walls, and e half-expected the tools to start flying for eir head.

"I'm sorry!" e said as an umpteenth drawer almost shut on eir fingers. "I know he's not here. I'm worried too, but I needed to bring Aliyah somewhere safe, all right?"

E'd set them down on their shared mattress, making sure the blankets and pillows were all properly arranged. Their breathing had turned uneven on the way back. Once, they'd jerked in Horace's arms then pressed a hand on eir face, as if to push em away. They'd moaned twice since, a long and plaintive sound that tore at Horace's heart. Whatever plagued their dreams didn't look pleasant.

At first, e sat by their side. Aliyah was clearly going through a hard time, and they should have someone there when they woke up. Besides, Keza had said to wait. So e should wait, right? But within an hour, the Wagon was slamming cupboards with such force one would think a thunderstorm was happening inside. The noise was awful and kept startling Horace. Eir heart wouldn't survive this, and it couldn't be any good for Aliyah either. Frustrated and exhausted, e threw eir arms up.

"All right, all right! I'm going." The Wagon immediately stopped its ruckus. "Just let me make a meal and shove it in the cold box, so Aliyah doesn't have to struggle through some feverish cooking."

When Horace clambered down the ladder, e found all the kitchen drawers open in invitation.

E set to work, heating up dried tomatoes with oil and the last fish left in the cold box. The familiarity of cooking eased eir nerves, calming eir frantic heart and the building anger. Or perhaps that was just the absence of Wagon-induced cacophony. It gave em space to think, and from there eir excitement blossomed, a guilty but undeniable thrill.

No way to obey the Wagon but to follow Keza, right? She'd said to wait, but patience had never been Horace's strength. Eir curiosity, however … that grew with every passing second. Besides, e was worried about Rumi. They didn't know Keza all that well, and she'd sounded like she'd meant to leave him to die before she'd dashed off with him. Surely she had a plan, something she didn't want em to learn. Again. But Horace couldn't just sit here for who-knew-how-many hours—or even days!—twiddling eir thumbs and hoping for the best. Aliyah was safe and had a meal in case they woke up. Nothing kept em in the Wagon, so Horace picked up Keza's staff and tied it across eir back, eir own sword and shield at the ready.

E plunged back into the now-familiar tunnels, following the patterns of glowing moss to the waterway room, in part guided by the rush of water along its canals. In the tank, a healthy flow drained through Rumi's dome, and the level had lowered enough in the big bulb that it no longer spilled from the upper crack. E wondered how fast the flooded pass would clear itself. A problem for later, that; first, e needed to track Keza down.

She couldn't have run that far, considering how wounded Rumi had been. There must be something down that other tunnel—something she'd meant to keep from all of them. Horace stared at the opening, eir throat tight. What if there were more Fragments there? How would e defend emself? E hoped what meagre sword and shield skills e had would serve, because no one was around to save em. E had never wandered in the wild alone before.

With a final deep breath, Horace ventured down the tunnel taken by Keza. E set a determined pace, squinting in the near-darkness. The moss here had died out, and only the rare blue flowers on their strange, twisting vines emitted any light. E trailed eir fingers on the wall to help situate emself, cursing eir lack of foresight. A torch would have been great! Keza might see fine in pitch black, but eir eyes weren't meant for it. Eir pace slowed, and when e reached an intersection, eir heart sank.

Right. Nothing had promised a straight line. How was e supposed to navigate this place? Did Keza just know it? Horace peered into the dark, squinting as if the rare blue glow revealed answers. What a pickle. If Keza had been through, there must be a trace e could follow, *something*.

Eir eyes caught a glimmer on the ground—blue light reflecting into shallow liquid. Eir heart stopped and e ran forward, to crouch and examine it. *Water*. Of course. Keza had been drenched from her time in the basin and the water collapsing on them, and Rumi was bleeding. Even with the spare hours between them, they both must have left little pools, and these corridors remained very humid. It'd take a while for anything to dry.

E hurried down the path, kneeling every few

paces to pat the stone ground and make sure e could still find wet puddles. More than once, e crouched so fast that the butt of Keza's staff hit the floor, and e cringed and froze, as if she'd leap from the shadows and scold em for not caring properly for her weapon. Every blue vine flower gracing em with light was a blessing, sparing eir back and knees.

Horace had no idea how long e continued this—time slowed and jellied in the dark—but when e finally caught a glimmer of a different pale light, eir muscles hurt from the constant bending, and e must have taken four turns, none of which e could remember. If e'd been wrong and this hadn't been the path, e was lost for good.

Horace hurried towards the light, eager to be out of these tunnels. With every step, e grew more convinced this led outside. The light had that natural quality to it that made em break into a run, grinning and squinting until e rounded a last corner and emerged outside.

A warm gust of wind hit em, tousling eir curls, and Horace burst out laughing. Eir booming voice echoed on the surrounding cliffs, melody to eir ears, and as eir sight readjusted, what breath e'd left vanished.

E stood on the upper section of a lush valley, nestled between two stiff mountain flanks. Water gushed out of the rock face on eir right, sprinting and leaping down the ledges and into a deep pool from which three grooves had been carved. It was far below, and distance blurred the details, but Horace traced the water as it wound its way through several plots of land cleverly irrigated by its flow. And now that e'd spotted those, eir eyes started to distinguish green-roofed structures scattered around the valley, camouflaged by the healthy shrubs and trees, and the path of flat stones between them.

A village. There was a village down there.

This had to be Keza's home! The water coursing to it, the need for food, it all made sense! And if she had a whole community nearby, then they probably had healers, too.

Horace sprinted forward, bounding down the steep and narrow path. E often tripped, slapping eir palm on the cliffside on eir left to keep eir balance. Once, eir momentum carried em so fast e had to jump to a large, flat boulder to stop before e lost complete control. Horace slowed after that. It didn't do anyone any good if e got emself killed. Especially if e broke Keza's staff on the way down. Still, big strides only! E wanted to get there as soon as possible, and hopefully be by Rumi's side when he woke up.

The path wound its way down in a tortuous string, sometimes leaving the flank to dip into a fissure in the mountain. As e slipped in its shadows, Horace began to ponder if Keza had carried all the crates down one by one, or if they had some secret platform to help, the way Trenaze moved large amount of goods between plateaus.

A small pebble tumbled at eir feet, sliding from the cliff on eir right. Instincts registered the swift motion that followed, the loud scrapping of claws on rocks, and e spun about, shield raised, just in time to deflect a spear aimed at em. The force staggered em backward, and in the time e needed for balance, two more assailants had dropped down, blocking both sides of the pass. Three felnexi, all with long pointed spears and a wary look. Horace had gotten eir ass handed to em hard enough by Keza to know where this was going. E threw eir hands up, the sword still in its scabbard.

"I don't have any food!" e said. "Sorry."

Eir stomach grumbled at the mention. How long had e been gone from the Wagon? E really should have brought something to eat.

"We don't care about your food," one retorted, with the same rolling accent as Keza's. They had great long fur with tortoise patterns, so thick near their nose it fell on both sides like a moustache. "Let's kill them, Nene. If they're here, they know too much."

They had turned towards the first felnexi dropping on Horace, with a short black coat and eyes blue as the sky. Nene hissed slowly, danger in every note of the sound. Panic gripped Horace's lungs and compressed em.

"Killing? I, hum—introductions first, perhaps?" A nervous laugh followed eir babbling. They all glared at em, but e couldn't stop the words spilling out. "I'm Horace ka-Zestra, and I use e/em pronouns. I came with Keza? Keza Nesmit?" Hurriedly, e reached for the staff on eir back. It stayed tangled in the straps, but after some fumbling e managed to bring it forward. "See, I even have her staff!"

Before Horace could blink, Nene had their spear at eir throat. The tip dug in, and Horace was acutely aware of the single blood droplet running down eir neck. So much for friendliness.

"I knew it," Nene growled. "How many of you?"

"I—just me! I mean, Aliyah's back at the Wagon, but they're not coming. I only—"

"Silence," the long-furred one snapped. "Nene, you know the rules."

They had rules about killing outsiders? Horace couldn't believe it. Why would anyone do that? "I-I can go back. I just wanted to make sure Rumi was all right. Little isixi? Keza would've brought him, I think?"

They stared at one another, one with their lips pulled back in a growl, the two others with aggressive twitches of their tails. Horace did eir best to stay very frozen and very non-threatening, even though e was bigger than all of them. Was this it, then? Would Aliyah wake up alone in an angry, worried Wagon, and never see any of them again? No wonder Keza hadn't wanted to tell them anything about this place.

Nene made a low, curling noise of frustration, then withdrew their spear. "Keza kicked the rules so far down the cliffs, we might as well follow. Bring em. We'll let the elders decide eir fate alongside everything else."

Relief washed through Horace, and e allowed emself to relax despite the two weapons still directed at em. At least they weren't at eir throat. "Oh, thank you! I am sorry for all the trouble. I didn't mean to—I didn't even know—"

Nene interrupted em with a sharp hiss. "Keep those lips shut, Horace ka-Zestra, and don't thank me yet."

Well, that was a little foreboding. Horace couldn't help eir pout. E wanted to talk with them! Sure, they were abrasive and had threatened to kill em, but they had this whole secret village, nestled in a beautiful valley and hidden in the mountains. How amazing was that? Eir questions would have to wait, though.

For now, e tried to contain the rising mix of excitement and fear as three Felnexi herded em towards their long-concealed home.

They walked em out of the fissure, down the twisting path, and to the village's gate—an archway carved in stone, above which the waterway passed, and from which long vines dropped, covering the opening and adorning it in blue flowers. Or, well, Horace thought of this as the entrance—it was a door, after all—but e'd spotted several caves with the same moss-and-engraving swirling designs as those on the mountain. Were those more habitations, perhaps for isixi or dwarven residents? It had taken at most forty minutes between Horace's quick sprint and the guarded trek to come down from the tunnels, and Horace wondered if these had all been connected, once upon a time.

The village itself was a gathering of sporadic structures either integrated into the rocks, or with flat roofs with their own small gardens. Many houses hugged trees and were built halfway up them, almost impossible to spot through the branches, and it felt to Horace as though most of the forest had been left intact while habitations sprawled through it. The streets were deserted, save for the occasional blur of fur slipping into doors or tails disappearing around a corner. E could sense the eyes tracking em, though, wary and curious. Once, e caught a pair in the foliage of a tree, and waved. They vanished in a rustle of leaves.

Horace was escorted to a long awning surrounding a much smaller house, all nestled between two big trees. It sported a clay oven and seats woven from branches and it all looked incredibly cozy in the setting sunlight, but just as Horace turned to ask about it, a felnexi opened the door and Nene shoved em in there. Horace blinked hard in the changing light, trying to readjust to the darkness, when a familiar voice greeted em.

"What in the cursed stars are you doing here?"

"Oh, hi, Keza!" e chirped.

She was sitting on a ledge near the ceiling, tail drooping towards the ground.

"Enjoy the company, Keza." Nene's tone dripped with hostility, but it had a layer of intimacy to it, of betrayal. Horace's gaze flicked between the two of them, picking up on the intensity of the shared glare. "You wanted it in our village so badly."

"Nene, wait!"

Keza leaped down, but her forward movement was halted short by Nene's sharp "Don't." Keza stopped at Horace's side, and e couldn't remember ever seeing so much tension in her. Every muscle had gone rigid, ready to spring. Nene averted their gaze and turned away, slamming the door behind them.

Horace and Keza stood in silence. Light filtered in from ill-fitting planks, bringing clouds of dust in keen relief. The room had two old straw mattresses, a few woven chairs and a table, but not much else for furniture. No windows, either. Horace doubted people lived here.

Keza still hadn't moved. Horace hated seeing

her like that, rigid and hurt. Because that had to be it, hurt, the way she stared at the door Nene had closed, the slight hunch in her shoulders.

"I, huh … brought your staff back?" e said quietly, extending it.

"I told you to wait!" Keza snapped, whirling on em. "You don't have to be the brightest star in the sky to follow that instruction."

Her fur had risen, puffing menacingly, and Horace reflexively slid a step back. But Keza was being unfair. E crossed eir arms and squared eir shoulders, holding eir ground.

"You left with my wounded friend, with no explanation about your intentions, seconds after telling me to forget saving him," Horace pointed out. "If you wanted me to wait, you should've said more!"

"I couldn't," Keza hissed. "Don't you get that yet? This place's a secret. We haven't had an outsider in hundreds of years!"

"And that would have been enough." Horace shoved the staff into her chest, dropping it. Keza caught it before it fell, scowling at em, but e didn't yield. "We all understood you had a secret. All I wanted was to know Rumi was safe. I was worried, and the Wagon was throwing a fit."

Keza huffed, but it was the last vestige of her rage. She spun about, pacing the room, and some of the stiffness left her muscles. "Well. Welcome to the land of the doomed."

And just like that, Horace's anger vanished as well, draining out of em like the water after Rumi had blown up the clog.

"Oh. Are-are you all cursed?" e asked, voice dropping into a terrified whisper.

Keza stared at em long and hard, and her lips pulled back, showing sharp teeth—then she burst into that quick and easy laugh Horace had grown so familiar with over the last days.

"You're serious, aren't you?" she asked between fits of laughter. "No, no, Horace. I meant you and I, not the whole place."

Horace didn't know whether to be disappointed, relieved, or worried. At least not everyone was cursed! But Keza didn't seem particularly optimistic about their future. It probably had to do with the secret thing, but e didn't understand why that doomed them.

"I can keep a secret. I swear I'll never say a word about this place."

"Yeah, this village didn't stay hidden for centuries by relying on people's good faith." She shifted from pacing to her fighting routine, and every strike of the staff seemed to relax her further. "They take deadlier means. Quick shove off the waterfall we brought back, for a start."

"But why?" Horace swept eir arm in the water's general direction, beyond the wall. "We helped! You need the water for the gardens, no? That's what this was all about."

"Yes," she confirmed, "and all of us unblocking that would have been all right until I came bounding down the cliff with shortscales." She stopped moving and sighed heavily, then turned to em. "The shit I got for that alone could clog the waterways all over again, but I figured, hey, he was out cold when I brought him, maybe I can convince everyone it'll be fine if we knock him out or blind him on the way out. Worth the risk."

Aw, Rumi would love to learn she liked him enough to take that risk. Maybe. He'd be less irritated at her all the time, at least, right? Or it'd balance that part about the knocking him out again. Horace thought so. And then e thought about what else she'd just implied, and eir stomach fell into eir heels.

"Oh."

"You bet, 'Oh'." Keza snapped.

Horace hadn't come in blindfolded. E'd found eir way through the maze of tunnels to their village. Not that e could pull that off again without the wet tracks, but the rest of Keza's folks didn't know that. If they wouldn't take eir word as good enough for an oath of secrecy, they wouldn't take it for this, either.

"What now?"

"I don't know," Keza admitted, and she let herself collapse by the wall, bringing her legs back to her, staff lazily set down by her side. "I don't think anyone knows, not even the elders."

"Rumi's safe, at least," Horace said. "Right?"

"Yeah." A smile flitted across her face, and she leaned against the wall. "Don't know when he'll wake up, but they got to him in time. Though if we're dead, he might be, too."

"Right." Horace slid down a spot near the

wall next to her. "So we just wait?"

"Unless you brought your children's game with you."

Horace laughed and shook eir head. "I didn't think I'd need saira here. The light's going away fast, anyway."

The sun had to be hiding behind the mountains, vanishing early compared to when it would have in Trenaze. Horace didn't mind. It had been a long day, between the bomb, the Fragments, Rumi's wounds, the Wagon's fit, then tracking Keza here. E closed eir eyes and shifted until the wood against eir back felt somewhat comfortable. E hoped Aliyah would be all right if they woke up with only a meal. When they'd absorbed the Fragments in Trenaze, they'd required a few hours to regain consciousness, but after the Dead Archives it had taken days. Horace had no idea how long they'd need to recover this time, and e wished e could be by their side.

Every now and then, Keza's tail flicked and brushed against em. At least e wasn't alone—and neither was Keza, now. Horace wondered if she found it as comforting as e did.

"Hey, Keza…" E hesitated, then turned to her. Deep orange cat eyes stared right back, and for a moment the words lumped in eir throat. E cleared it. "You think… You think you could teach me a few things? About fighting."

Her ears twitched, but she smiled at em. "Won't do you much good if they need us both dead, but sure. You could use some pointers."

Horace laughed. E wasn't about to debate that. "Great. Really great, even. I guess if I'm to die soon, it'd be at least one thing I wanted before I go."

The constant rustle of Keza's tail stopped for an instant, and Horace froze with it. Was that too much? E hadn't meant to be so sentimental. E was about to fumble eir way through some dampening of eir words when a low, regular rumble filled the room. Purring. Horace grinned, sinking into the quiet and warmth of the sound, so unusual from Keza.

6

The Young and the Old

They rose long before the sun, and in the darkness Keza trained Horace's ears and reflexes. She stalked around em, her claws barely scratching the ground with every stride, biding her time and rushing em at random intervals. Horace's job was to spin about with eir shield to block her open palm, reacting only to the slight scrape of her claws from her dash. E rarely moved quick enough. Keza was fast and silent, deadly in darkness her eyes easily pierced. Still, eir performance the second day *had* improved, insofar as e parried her a grand total of four times over two hours of training. Better than none.

Once dawn peeked through the planks, they worked on eir stances. Keza showed em new positions to reinforce eir flexibility and corrected eir others—apparently e had been doing em wrong, but either eir Clan Zestra's *nes* hadn't noticed, or they hadn't bothered to tell em. The first, probably. Surely they hadn't given up on Horace before e had even really started, right? Surely not. But e did have quite the reputation, in Trenaze. No one else had failed as many apprenticeships in recent memory; no one else had lingered as a *ka* for so long.

It didn't matter, not anymore. Horace did eir best to bury the nagging self-doubt. E'd found eir place by Aliyah's side, and now e'd found someone who believed in em, even if only for a few days, before their joint execution. In fact, e decided to take Keza's willingness to fix eir mistakes despite the inevitable end as proof she thought it worthwhile.

Deprived of Horace's sword, they focused on hand-to-hand combat and general posture, spending most of the afternoons on it. The inch of Horace's body spared from bruises in the morning did not escape Keza over the course of *that* part, and on the first day, after a few hours of gruelling fighting, e had collapsed on the ground, panting.

"I'm only good at taking the hits, huh?" e asked, dizzy from the all-body throbbing.

Eir eyes traced cracks in their stone ceiling to keep eir vision from unfocusing—until Keza leaned right above em, grinning.

"Not gonna deny it's helping my mood to pummel you, but you're too hard on yourself. You learn fast."

She extended a hand to haul em up, but Horace only stared at it and her in confusion. "I do?"

"Sure." She clasped eir forearm and heaved em up without waiting for em. It startled Horace, and e belatedly sat, going with her pull. "I keep having to change tactics to hit you. Don't you even realize that? I use an opening once or twice, and you're already rushing to cover it in our next spar. Most trainees don't know to try until you point out where the flaw is."

Horace let that sink in. E definitely had *not* realized that. Fights with Keza felt like a desperate scramble, not a calculated attempt to block her attacks. But she'd know better, right? E grinned and massaged eir pecs, where she'd struck a few times in the last rounds.

"Can't wait for it to pay off."

Keza laughed, and e was about to join in when Nene flung the door open. They stood in the entrance, the sun's backlight making their fur even darker, and their presence sapped all mirth from Keza. She turned rigid again—poised, Horace thought, although for a blow or a chance to attack, e couldn't tell.

"I was informed you were to carry out your duties even while waiting for the Council," they said.

Keza's eye slits widened, and for a second it felt like her entire body slackened and she'd fall to the ground, but she caught herself. When she spoke, her voice still held the shock.

"By whom? Lena?"

Not just shock; hope, too, in the curl of love with which she pronounced Lena's name. The same she used for Nene's, full of yearning and fear and tangled emotions.

"Lena doesn't decide for all of us," Nene

retorted, and their deep frown lessened. A hint of mirth crawled into their voice. "The little ones do."

Nene stepped aside, and a veritable tide of fur and claws rushed through the door, screaming. Seven—no, nine—felnexi children scrambled inside, climbing on top of one another as they squeezed through the opening, some yowling as their peers stomped over their head, others giggling with glee as they did the stomping. A thin black kid slipped in front of the crowd, threw their arms open, and yelled "Keza!!"

Keza bent to greet them, arms open and face lit by a wide grin different from her usual smirks, deep and vulnerable. The child pounced on her, and she spun them about. She'd only done half a turn by the time the others caught up, climbing on her with their claws out, clamouring for attention. A veritable army of grey and black and orange fur, all big-eared and big-eyed. Keza brought the first black-furred kid into her arms and touched as many others as she could with her free hands, laughing.

"Calm down, calm down! I'm not going to vanish."

One of them—a cat with a deep burned orange fur and a face far more triangular than their peers—stepped back, tail flicking angrily. "But you did."

Guilt flashed across Keza's expression and she grimaced. "I'm sorry, Ella. I didn't mean to."

"Nene said to say goodbye at the end today," another piped up—the smallest of them, all in very fluffy grey fur and with their tail cut short. "That you'd be going somewhere again."

Horace and Keza both turned towards the entrance, but Nene was long gone, door closed behind them. Keza stared at it, but the children kept pulling at her clothes, claws leaving tiny holes in them. One of them had managed to climb onto her shoulders and head and had their feet deep in her back. Horace couldn't help thinking that must hurt.

"I don't know yet," she said, at length. "Not by choice."

"Mama Keza, who's this?"

The question came from the head-perched child, whose eyes—the same orange and shape as Keza's—had latched onto em. If Keza looked relieved by the change of topic, Horace instead found emself pinned by nine pairs of eyes, with expression ranging from wary to excited curiosity.

"A friend," Keza answered, and Horace couldn't stop eir huge grin. Friend! She rolled her eyes. "Eir name is Horace ka-Zestra, with e/em pronouns. E helped bring the water back."

There was a chorus of "oooooo" and "hello Horace", with a single, high-pitched voice that went "e/em, got it!", and Horace just about melted into the floor. E waved at the group.

"It's a pleasure to meet you," e said.

Several of the little ones turned back to Keza, then, and one asked "Can we?"

Keza caught Horace's eyes, and her fond smirk returned in full force. Mischief dripped from her tone as she set the child in her arms down amongst their peers.

"Oh, but Horace would *love* to play with all of you. I don't think e knows Tallest Branch."

"Tallest—"

Horace never got to finish eir question. Nine little felnexi leaped and pounced and sprinted, trampling over one another to get to em first—

then, as e raised a feeble arm in protest, they sprang to it, claws out, and started climbing. Horace winced at the prickles of pain and threw a confused look at Keza, who only extended her two arms out … and imitated a tree? E followed suit as more and more of the little ones buried em under their onslaught, scaling eir legs and chest and arm and head, pushing and pulling each other to be the one on top.

It was in many ways a horribly painful experience, but the constant stream of laughs and victorious screams helped ease the discomfort. So did Keza's relaxed, half-lidded gaze as she watched, perched once more on a high ledge, and the subtle purr e sometimes caught amidst the chaos.

E got into the game, playing eir part as the tree. First e leaned to one side, creating a new highest point with a raised hand, and enjoyed the panicked scramble across eir shoulders as the children tried to reach it. Later, e declared loudly "Oh no, there's a lot of wind today" and shook first eir arms, then eir whole body, forcing them to cling or fall. They loved every minute of it, and so did Horace.

In time, however, Horace's arms grew heavy, and the little ones didn't strive for eir head or raised hands with as much energy. E picked the current winner—a three-coloured cutie with almost round ears—and set them on the ground, lowering emself in the process and sitting in the middle of these nine incredible kids. E had no idea how long they'd played, but the sunlight had taken the reddish quality of impending sunset. Keza slipped down from her perch, landing with a soft thump.

"Come on now, let me see you all," she said, joining the group.

She yanked one up by the neck, placed them on her lap, and began what felt like a routine examination, poking at their ears, lifting their arms, and picking dirt from their furs with her claws. The first one submitted moodily, and once Keza released them, they hopped away and to the other side of Horace's bulk, lowering themself to the ground.

All other eight children tensed. Keza's gaze danced from one to the other—then the Tallest

Branch winner darted away. Keza laughed and caught them before they could get out of range.

"Darling, you should know better."

Horace watched as Keza went through all her litter, cleaning them one by one. It was slow and intimate in a way e hadn't expected from her, yet she did it all with a loving roughness e recognized, and which made it all the more precious. E kept eir silence, seeing in the moment the same precious ephemeral beauty as the brief show of lights from the Fragments mist before it'd vanished. By the end, most of the small felnexi were nestled against Horace, relaxed but for the wary eye they kept on Keza. Little by little, however, that last resistance dispersed, and they fell asleep, nine bundles of warmth clustered together. One had his hands wrapped around Horace, the half-out claws prickled at eir skin. Horace closed eir eyes, basking in the tenderness of it all, and time slipped away.

"It's the best, isn't it?"

Keza's wistful whisper startled em. She was sitting with three of her children draped over her crossed legs, face tilted up in a rare beam of moonlight. E must have dozed off.

"Y-yeah. Like cradling a sleeping baby but … more of them." E kept eir chuckle to a minimum, afraid to disturb the slumbering felnexi. "I've been around lots of children back home, but the cuddle piles were rare accidents."

"You're missing out."

"Not gonna argue with that."

E thought of the shared mattress with Aliyah, of holding them every night through nightmares and peaceful dreams, of falling asleep and waking up to their warmth. Shared beds in Trenaze were usually a matter of convenience, not an exchange of trust and warmth.

"I'm glad they let me have it one last time," she said, before extirpating herself from under the sleeping children. "They're coming, Horace. The Council of Elders meets at night."

They met at night, in the centre of the village,

where the forest had grown thick and ominous, encircling a small clearing, dark branches stretching overhead and concealing all but a few stars. What the canopy did not devour, the steep mountains did, until it felt to Horace as though the deep shadows around em threatened to engulf em. They weighed on eir lungs, stealing eir breath, and all e could think to do was slide closer to Keza.

They had been escorted from their holding house by the same felnexi who had first taken Horace on eir way down into the valley. Nene hadn't said anything to Keza, and they walked at the front now, hands tight on their spear, ears flat, tail swishing in slow and stiff movements. Keza only stared at them, as if nothing else mattered. Only once they reached the clearing did Nene turn around, and for a brief moment their eyes met. The silence felt so charged Horace expected it to spark.

Nene left without a word, following the two other warriors out, and Keza closed her eyes. Horace leaned in, stretching a finger to touch her forearm—only the one, and only the tip. A smile brushed her lips, and she nodded at em.

A single green flame flared to life at the centre of the clearing. Its dim light danced across an ancient, moss-covered stone platform, but it didn't reach far beyond, touching the surrounding branches only in flickering, frightened moments. Eir throat had gone dry, eir palms sweaty. Every rustle in the branch set eir nerves ablaze. Above, a pair of feline eyes caught the light, reflecting it briefly before vanishing amongst the foliage.

"Keza Nesmit, Master of the Inae Dance, Mother of Nine, you stand before the Council of Elders."

The deep voice surged from the shadows, and Horace spun on emself, desperate to pinpoint it. Everywhere, e found slit eyes staring back, and once e thought e distinguished thick moustaches, but never more.

"Keza," the voice continued, growing both softer and angrier at once. "We have met countless times to discuss your disregard for our rules and customs, and excused them in light of your exceptional skills. But you have gone too far."

The voice was a thunderstorm, looming and dangerous, ready to flood their lives and sweep them away. Horace remembered Keza's talk of a deadly waterfall plunge and swallowed hard. E wished e could see the shapes in the shadows, that these elders seemed less otherworldly.

Keza did not have that problem.

"Yeah, yeah, I've heard it all before." She stretched besides em, all lazy bravado. "No offence, Elder Miho, but I've seen you get fur caught in your throat in broad daylight, so this set-up's nowhere near as spooky as you'd like."

Horace almost choked at the level of disrespect and whirled on Keza. Did she want to get them killed? Keza grinned shamelessly at em before unhooking her staff and leaning on it. It triggered a series of hisses and growls from the canopy.

"You've been debating this infraction for two days. What am I supposed to do? Plead? Cower? Come on now. I know your minds are made up."

"An apology would have been a welcome start," a new voice said, velvet against the night.

"Are you not ashamed of what you've done, Keza Nesmit?"

This time, Keza laughed—but Horace had already been around her enough to pick up the bitter strain in it, and e was not surprised by its abrupt end, or the quiet fury that burned in eir friend afterwards.

"I'm not. We would have starved. Lena is sick. My children need this food to grow happy and healthy. Everything else is secondary." She tapped the staff on the ground and gave it a quick whirl. "What's the point of the Inae tradition if we all die upholding its secrets?"

Silence followed, so complete and heavy that Horace held eir breath for fear of breaking it. Keza was staring up and ahead, at what e presumed was one of the elders. E still couldn't pinpoint them.

"Very well," Elder Miho said. The finality of their tone did not bode well. "Your lack of remorse only bolsters our decision. Understand, Keza Nesmit, that your companions will share your fate."

Keza offered the slightest nod in response,

and the canopy rustled, pleased by her acceptance. Horace's heart shot all the way up to eir throat.

"W-Wait! Don't I get a say in this? I have regrets!"

Keza choked down a laugh by eir side, but she didn't turn to face em. Since none of the elders instructed em to shut up either, Horace forged onward.

"Look, I just—I didn't even know I wasn't allowed here! Keza didn't tell me this existed, or how to get to it. I did that all on my own, and I sure couldn't do it again. Or find my way out, actually." This time, e was certain Keza was laughing. Which, *fair*, maybe. E was gesticulating, and not very coherent, but also all these elders were casually talking about killing them or whatnot. "I just wanted Rumi to be safe. I still want Rumi to be safe. I don't think any of us deserves to die for that."

"Die?" That was the velvet voice, the one who'd wanted Keza to apologize. "No, we have a fate much worse for you in mind."

A sharp laugh behind Horace startled em, and

e whirled around in time to catch blue eyes mirror the torchlight. E slunk back, closer to Keza.

"Like w-what? Eternal Fragment possession?"

E couldn't think of anything else worse than *that*, which also felt like an infinitely cruel fate to bestow upon anyone. They couldn't mean that … could they? E glanced at Keza, hoping for reassurance, and caught understanding blooming on her face.

"You mean me, don't you?" she asked, her gaze latched on something in the darkness, the elder with the velvet voice Horace couldn't see. "I'm being exiled. With them."

"You cannot stay here," Elder Miho confirmed.

"And you cared enough for their lives to break our greatest taboo," continued the second known voice.

"Consider it a favour," a third raspy voice added.

Horace had not heard this one before and instantly disliked it. It had a haughty, mocking tone, like it relished the tension growing in Keza's shoulders and the tightness of her voice. Keza did not turn to face it, but the angry flick of her tail told Horace all e needed.

"Because I'm not dead, Elder Mawar?"

Elder Mawar did not stick to the darkness, as had the others. They dropped from above, a dark grey shadow landing near Horace and Keza. They were tall—taller than even Horace—their limbs all irate angles, almost reminiscent of the jagged edges of Fragments. When they stalked forward, eyes unreadable from reflected moonlight, Horace slid a step backwards. Keza held her ground.

"Not you, not these filthy outsiders you've brought to us, and not your name." They set a claw under Keza's chin, forcefully turning it. Her ears lowered but she didn't fight back, only bared her teeth as Elder Mawar continued, voice dropping into a whisper. "You'll leave with honour when your name should've been struck from our histories, forgotten except in dark legends that serve as warnings. It pains me, and were I as undisciplined as you, I might disregard my colleague's decision and bring my own punishment to the table, but alas…" Elder Mawar released her with a flick, and Horace would've sworn the claw had left a scratch. "I'll soothe that particular discontent watching your children grow up without your terrible influence, I suppose."

There was no mistaking the low growl vibrating out of Keza, nor the slight shift in her balance—a position to strike. Horace touched her elbow right as she brought the staff to bear, and she froze, russet fur on end. Elder Mawar had slunk a few elegant paces away but stopped at the audible threat behind them to look over their shoulder and smirk. Keza, miraculously, did not pounce on them.

"Then I suppose I'll soothe my discontent with the knowledge that I'm to thank for every meal you'll have until death finally reaps you. May awareness of that turn sweet tomatoes to bitter ash on your tongue, may the waterways forever whisper my name, and may you never know peace under the stars. Horace?" She spun to em, then, the fury of her curse still fresh on her face. "Let's get Rumi and leave. Now."

She stalked away, head held high, giving Elder Mawar no time to react. Horace watched her vanish into the shadows, took one step to follow, then turned around. Elder Mawar was gone, no doubt lurking in the canopy above with the others. E had never mastered the art of sweeping departure, and words jostled at eir lips.

"Well, it was huh … a pleasure? I think? Goodnight, anyway. May the glyphs—or stars or whichever—bless you."

With an awkward chuckle and an even more awkward bow, e spun on eir heels and hurried after Keza, leaving the flame-lit clearing and its moonshine eyes behind.

7

Departure

The rest of the village didn't sport creepy flickering green flames and enfolding darkness. A string of golden bulbs lit the path from above, and it took a ridiculous amount of squinting and staring before Horace figured out they were stretched, ballooned bioluminescent mushrooms tied with the same filaments. They hung from branches like a scattering of minuscule suns, blessing the front of a few houses with their glow. In between those pockets, however, Horace had only the stars' light as eir guide. Had it not been for them, e might have walked through the entire area without noticing most of the doorways and windows blended with the surrounding nature.

Keza never slowed, eyes fixed forward, each

stride fast and determined. More than once, Horace lagged behind to soak in the village and found emself scanning the starlit paths ahead for her lean shape. At least eir long legs helped em catch up. No one came out to watch them, let alone greet them. Horace wondered what they thought of Keza, if they even knew what she'd done for them or the price she paid for it. This seemed a small community. Surely word had spread?

Lost in eir thought, e bumped into Keza, startling both of them. She glared at em but raised a hand to stall any apology. "Wait here."

Then she was gone, climbing up a tree and into the dark canopy above. Horace stared until e could distinguish the lines of a building, the contour of a door. If Keza moved about the house, e could not hear. E had no doubts, however, that nine small felnexi slept within, heaped together in a mound of fuzzy warmth.

Keza dropped back in front of em within a few minutes—too fast for goodbyes. She had a bag slung over her shoulder. Horace's chest ached from the idea of her packing in the dead of the night, sweeping a few essentials before she vanished forever. She lifted a single object for em to see, a bunch of coloured sticks tied together by a piece of bark.

"More children's games," she said, "to pass the time. Got the two cards you dropped, too."

Stealing games without a word of permission, as e had weeks ago in Trenaze. E could have laughed, but this might be one of the few mementos Keza preserved of this place and, unlike em, she'd never get to go home. Eir sadness must have shown on eir face, because she scowled at em.

"Let's make one thing clear: my life here is over. What you saw of it, of me, of the village? You keep it to yourself."

"All of it?"

The slight throb of a hundred tiny scratches as toddlers climbed all over em hadn't vanished. The memory of them sleeping piled on em never would. E couldn't believe Keza wanted to erase that when she'd given everything for it.

"All of it." Her voice broke no disagreement, but after a moment she cracked a grin at em. "Except the training, of course. I hope you're ready to get your ass beat a lot more."

Horace laughed this time, but eir heart wasn't into it. E wanted to wrap her in a big hug and tell her it was all right to mourn her family, that this exile was cruel. E didn't think it'd be welcome.

"Always," e said instead.

That was the end of it. Keza's smile turned to its usual smirk, the one she wore like armour, and she brushed past em, leading the way deeper into the village.

The infirmary was in a cavern nestled in the mountain's side, its entrance covered with a curtain of vines and leaves, which rustled as they slipped through. An enormous splash of moss lit the cooler room within, and their soft green light granted Rumi's blue scales a dark teal. He was lying on a too-large bed placed against the far wall, a pile of clothes and random gear at its feet.

The moment they stepped in, Rumi sprang into action.

From his seemingly sleeping position, he spun on the bed and flung an arm out, as if aiming at them. There was a small contraption in his hands, and Horace's heart leaped into eir throat as it *thwacked* and—broke? Something snapped and flew backward, smacking Rumi's snout in full force. He yelped in pain and threw it to the ground with a curse.

"Rumi!" E launched forward, worry squeezing eir chest.

"H-Horace?" Rumi's eyes widened as he took them both in, panting. He rubbed his nose where it'd been struck, grimacing. "I didn't think it'd be you!"

"Was that meant to hurt us?" Keza asked, eyebrows raised.

Rumi hissed at her. "I built it with what I had at hand."

Namely, rough strings, snapped pieces of wood, bandage wrapping, and other parts Horace couldn't identify.

"As resourceful as ever. It's good to see you alive," Horace put in, interrupting before they could bicker. "Can you walk, Rumi?"

The more e looked at him, the less likely that seemed. A scraggly line crossed his chest where the Fragment shard had stabbed him, and his eyes had sunk in. Even the flicks of his tail had slowed, as if all of Rumi's energy went into sitting upright.

"Of course I can walk!" he piped up. "I woke up from near death only a few hours ago and had to scrap together this baby, but I can walk for miles and miles if it means getting away from this place. They tried to tie me to the bed, can you believe it?"

Keza rolled her eyes and started away. "Pick him up, Horace. He's five minutes off from collapsing."

Horace had to agree with that assertion. E scooped Rumi up, careful not to squeeze him, and settled him on eir broad shoulders. When his friend's small claws reached through the curls to hold tight, the memories of nine children resurfaced, heavy in eir chest.

"Did you come to rescue me?" Rumi asked. "There's a meal at the Wagon, right? They barely gave me anything to eat, here. Everyone knows injured people need—"

"Hush, Rumi," Horace said firmly. E'd caught the sharp twitch of Keza's tail as she walked ahead. Every word out of Rumi's mouth must only deepen her wounds. "A lot happened."

Rumi leaned on eir head, his voice dropping to a whisper. "What's up with Keza? This is her home, isn't it? I can't get a rise out of her."

Ah, that was why he was being so loud about his discontent. Not that Rumi tended to keep his opinions to himself, but Horace had come to expect the positive ones first.

"This *was* her home," Horace said. E had promised not to overshare, but surely e could tell Rumi that much. He'd reach the conclusion on his own if Keza stayed with them. "They exiled her."

Rumi fell silent. They left the last few trees behind, and Horace focused on Keza's slinking shadow some distance ahead. The steep mountains cast their route in darkness, and e didn't want to lose sight of her. The number of handmade structures diminished, the occasional houses gave way to garden plots, and the cobbled paths turned into a stone trail, the last of the stringed lights vanishing. Horace was forced to slow eir pace to keep from stumbling on the uneven, rocky ground. Sometimes Rumi tapped eir shoulder to alert them to obstacles, but the small isixi stayed silent for the most part, and Horace had the distinct impression he was fighting the urge to doze off.

Hand on the sheer cliff at eir right, Horace followed the climbing trail as it took a deep bend and was suddenly cast in starlight. On the path ahead, Keza had stopped, surrounded by three other felnexi, including Nene. Horace froze, and when e felt Rumi shuffle and prepare to talk, e reached up and clamped eir friend's mouth shut.

They were close, intimately so. Keza had her forehead against another felnexi's, whose white fur glowed in the moon as if they were a single fat drop of light. Nene—slim and dark and so intimidating—had their fingers on Keza's cheek, gently, their eyes closed and their face locked into an expression of pain. The last had their tail entwined in Keza's legs and tail, a hand delicately in hers. Horace's chest ached as e watched them, their loss sweeping over em as surely as a rising tide, choking out eir breath. The first tears blurred eir sight as they broke it off.

Nene stepped back first, and their eyes flicked towards Horace. They whispered to Keza, words forever meant only for her, then all three felnexi retreated. They darted up the sheer cliff, claws digging into the rock, leaving Keza behind, a lonely figure, bright orange in the pale light.

Rumi clambered down Horace's back, landing with a clack of claws, but Keza didn't react, her gaze glued to the cliff her lovers had climbed. Slowly, his steps wobbly from exhaustion, he walked to her and placed a small hand on her wrist. She sighed, and finally looked at him.

"You're right, shortscales. Adventures await."

They still had to wait for the Inari Pass to drain out.

The first day had to be the quietest in Horace's life. Rumi slept for most of it, recovering from his wound, emerging from his bed only long enough to eat. Satisfied by his return, the Wagon had stopped its smashing of cupboards and drawers and gone fully still. Aliyah had yet to emerge from their Fragments-induced slumber, though they didn't toss about anymore. It left Horace and Keza, but after a morning training session, she'd vanished into the mountains for hours, reappearing with a mix of small game, herbs, and wild berries for em to cook. She didn't comment on Aliyah's extended sleep, didn't question how they'd met or where they were going, didn't take any interest in her new, forced companions.

Horace did eir best to give her the space she obviously needed. E valiantly didn't ask about her family or feelings, and while e inevitably rambled on about the beauty of the sky and mountain while they ate, filling in the otherwise intolerable silence, e didn't pressure her to answer or even pay attention. It was painful. Every inch of em screamed "New friend!" and longed for more.

E managed to hold it together for another day, but as the sun set behind the mountain range and shadows stretched across the desert landscape, e couldn't take it anymore.

"You should teach me your children's game," e told Keza. "After dinner."

She inclined her head in assent, and hours later they settled at the Wagon's table, the plates cleared. Horace had half-expected Keza to vanish before then, dodging any obligations to em, but instead she brandished the game like a weapon, her usual energy back in force.

"It's very simple. We call it the Thorny Bush."

Horace tended to have a different definition of simple than most, but e quieted eir doubts. Keza withdrew a bunch of sticks from their leather pouch and held them vertically in the middle of the table. Most of these were smooth, about six inches long with pointed ends, but some had retained the scraggly twists of natural twigs, with the offshoots filed off. Both the straight and bumpy sticks had been tinted in one of three colours: yellow, green, or red.

"All you gotta do is pick up the sticks without moving any others." Keza released them, and they fell onto the table in a messy, tangled pile, most still touching each other. "Yellow's one point, green is three, and red is five. Add one if they're twigs. You *can* use previous sticks as tools."

"That's unfair," Horace said. "There's no way I'll ever beat you at a game like this!"

It drew a sharp laugh out of her, and she gestured at the spread of twigs. "I'll let you start."

Horace's gaze snapped to the sticks that had rolled away from the pile and e snatched up a green stick that didn't touch anything before looking up at Keza. Too late, e realized e acted like a child seeking approval. She laughed once more.

"See? Simple. You can go again. As long as you don't move any other sticks."

So she'd let em get any sticks that were clear of others, as a head start. Horace obliged until e was forced to tackle the tangled pile itself. E snatched up a stick in precarious equilibrium at the top, then another. Eir grin widened as eir confidence grew—until e became too cocky and tripped not one, but three of them at once. Keza perked up, her ears twitching with alertness.

"Now it's my turn," she said.

She emptied half the Thorny Bush in a single turn, meticulously picking her way through the sticks, extracting the twisted twigs with care, or flipping those atop the pile with a flick of another stick. The agility and precision were a spectacle in and of themselves, and served as consolation for the obvious impeding loss. Still, when she made a mistake—and Horace wasn't certain she hadn't done it on purpose—e was eager to get eir chance at it.

Stick in hand, e targeted a red one at the edge, hoping to nudge it away with eir own, little by little. All of eir focus went into the act, eir entire world narrowing to the single red stick.

"New game?"

Aliyah's voice startled Horace—not only by its mere presence, but by the deep scratchiness of it. E whirled around, scattering the Thorny Bush.

Bark climbed along Aliyah's neck and cheek, spreading across a still-green eye. It covered the back of their hand, and their fingers stretched longer than normal. When had they transformed again? Horace had checked on them over and over, and they'd seemed fine aside from their agitated sleep.

"Aliyah! Are you all right?"

"I'm—" They stopped, gnarly fingers curling on themselves. "I am. But I must … they're—In the caverns, there is a place. Somewhere I must go."

Their voice ebbed in and out of the scratchy, powerful tone as they stumbled through their words. Drawn out by Aliyah's return, Rumi emerged from his room, tiny claws clinging to the curtain.

"Not sure that's a great idea," he said.

Horace agreed. Aliyah didn't seem healthy enough to em, not even remotely. All the tree stuff didn't help, but they also kept their jaw clenched and shoulders tight, as if holding out against pain.

"What kinda somewhere?" Keza asked, her tone tense despite her lazy posture on the chair.

"Not your people's village." Aliyah's stark dismissiveness drew a hiss out of Keza, but they didn't give her time to retort, turning to Horace instead. "Please."

E sprang to eir feet. "Of course I'm coming.

But you gotta eat while I get ready. There's a plate for you in the cold box still."

A sharp laugh escaped Aliyah, and some of the tension bled out of them. "You cooked for me. It is good to be back with you."

Horace retrieved eir dutifully prepared meal, and while Aliyah pecked at it, e donned eir leather armour and grabbed eir sword and shield. By the time e clambered back down the Wagon's ladder, most of Aliyah's plate was empty, and both Rumi and Keza stood ready by the exit. Warmth spread through Horace's chest. E grinned and clapped eir hands.

"Nothing like a mysterious group escapade!"

8

The Inae Tradition

Chill winds hit them as they stepped out under the shining stars, and a breeze tossed Horace's curls about. Eir gaze went straight to the expanse of the sky, so wide and pure above eir head, infinite. E'd never get tired of seeing it without Trenaze's pink domes curtailing its glory.

Rumi nudged em, drawing em out of eir reverie. Aliyah had already plunged back into the underground passages, followed by Keza, so Horace jogged after them, until Rumi complained at em to "wait up on his small legs and poor wounded body".

They returned to the great reservoir's room, but Aliyah didn't stop there, striding across its expanse to take another tunnel, passing through its archway without pause. Wood popped and cracked with their steps, the bark along their skin receding and growing, their shape ever-changing, sometimes almost completely human, sometimes more branches and roots than anything else. Horace's nerves tingled at their single-minded purpose as they traversed the moss-lined corridor, then turned into a set of narrow, upward circular stairs. E couldn't tell who was in control—Aliyah or the tree creature?—and e realized e'd never interrogated whether they were the same person. Worries formed about Fragments and possession and Aliyah's peculiar powers, which seemed to bloom around the golden shards—the very same they awakened, somehow. E couldn't put the fear into clear questions, but it tightened eir throat as e followed eir friend.

Aliyah led them into a cubic room packed with ... machinery? Six towering contraptions of stone and glass rose in every corner, as well as along the left and right walls, each reminiscent of the bulb reservoir, but with way more moving pieces. Or potentially moving pieces, at any rate. The gears and arms lay still, covered in dust, their purpose long forgotten.

The only motion came from the ceiling, where water flowed through a lengthy spiral glass funnel encased in glowing moss, and down into a tall cylindrical device in the middle. As Aliyah walked to it, new branches burgeoned out of their back, reaching for the ceiling as if to pull them up. Under them, roots elongated, keeping them anchored as they hung between the ceiling's pattern and the tube below. Bark grew over their entire face, both their eyes shining green, and when they spoke, it was with a fully eldritch voice.

"Something … broken."

"I'll find it," Rumi said. "I can totally find it!"

Rumi hopped into the room, awe filling his tone. He wove his way through Aliyah's roots and to the central device, pressing his snout against the old and thick glass to study it. After a few contemplative minutes, he turned to Horace. "Can you lift me? I want to see better."

The next hour was a cycle of Rumi poking and

humming and asking for physical help as he went around the room, following mechanisms only he understood. Keza paced the space, her tail flicking impatiently. At times, she stopped near the entrance, where a long vine of blue flowers clung to the wall, and traced their petals with the tip of her claws. Whatever she thought of this room, she kept it to herself.

When not called upon for eir height and muscles, Horace wandered towards the back wall, where a soft glow had caught eir attention. E quickly discovered it was not a wall, but a window, dirtied to the point of non-recognition by decades, if not centuries. Beyond, through the thick layer, e could distinguish the massive shape of the bulb reservoir covered in the dim, luminescent moss. When e remarked on it, Rumi nodded.

"I think this is some sort of control room for it? Not quite figured out the whole of it, but these—" He gestured to the big wheels at the foot of each of the six contraptions. "—are manual release. What for, though… Any helpful labels have been erased by time, and from what little of them I can make, it's not any language I know."

"Inner sanctum." Aliyah's scratchy voice startled them. Since arriving, they had been eerily still in the centre of the room, but now they pointed towards the cylinder. "Baths. Inner gardens. Training room. Valley. Overflow."

"How do you even *know* that?" Keza asked.

Her demand was full of sharp edges, but Aliyah ignored it. They stopped moving, a tree gone dormant. When Keza stepped forward with a growl, Rumi scoffed.

"There's no point," he said. "Aliyah knows things they shouldn't, and doesn't know things they should. That's just how it is."

Keza glared at him. "Because *you* accept it doesn't mean I have to."

"No, you'd rather cause problems while Aliyah and I work on fixing an issue that, as far as I can tell, only impacts *your* people. Colour me surprised."

For once, Keza had no good retort prepared. She threw her arms out and declared "I'm bored! This is excruciating." before storming out. Horace doubted boredom explained all her behaviour, but e didn't need to dig deep to uncover other reasons for her to be out of sorts. E'd left Trenaze—where e'd struggled to find eir place and people to belong with—of eir own volition, weeks ago now, and e still grappled with homesickness. Keza's exile had been imposed suddenly, and she'd barely said her goodbyes. She'd need time to heal from it.

"I can work in peace now, at least," Rumi said, but it had none of its usual bite.

"She'll be fine," Horace replied. "She goes out on her own a lot."

Rumi huffed, pretending he wasn't worried, but he stared at the door where Keza had vanished for a few seconds before returning to the cacophony of mechanisms to unravel. Horace grinned at his back, thrilled that for all his posturing, he was coming around to Keza.

Another hour ticked by, and Horace found emself sitting by the entrance, fighting the urge to doze off. The highlight of the last period had been a quick trip back to the Wagon to retrieve Rumi's tools. The small engineer's entire attention had turned to the central cylinder, which he'd deemed, 'the actual control' and 'some sort of clock'. None of his work drew a reaction from Aliyah until he leaped up with a triumphant exclamation.

"Now I get it! Wow, that's clever, and not too hard to fix, I'd think."

Aliyah dropped with a disturbing wooden crack, all her roots dissolving into pale green mist as they landed on top of it. "We should do it. It feels important."

They sounded more themself than they had since waking up, and Horace scrambled to eir feet. "Do you know why? What happened?"

"I dreamed of this place, dreamed of urgency, of disaster. It is … hard to explain. I had to come." Their gaze flickered around the room, their still-barked skin creaking as they frowned. "Keza left us?"

"Got bored. You know how she is," Rumi answered. "Doesn't matter. If I can bring this cylinder back to the Wagon, I can fix it. Not like I got anything better to do while we wait for the Pass to drain out."

Rumi slowly but surely disentangled the tube from the rest of the contraption, after which

Horace had to heave the massive piece of stone and glass all the way back to the Wagon. It barely fit through the door, and once set in the middle of Rumi's workshop, it felt even bigger. Keza had been waiting for them, perched in the rafters extending out of the second floor.

"So what is it?"

"A water hourglass," Rumi declared. "It tracks the passage of the year and closes the reservoir's grates according to needs." He pressed his hands against the thick glass to point at two inner containers linked by a small opening. "Water drips from one to the other through there, very slowly, but once it reaches a certain weight, it flips. Every flip hits this piece here, and that's recorded by this secondary mechanism, which turns with the hit."

"Get to the point?" Keza asked.

Rumi snapped his teeth at her. "I'll take all the time I want, thank you. But the *point* is that the counter mechanism is broken, so it wasn't telling the bottom grate—the one to your village—to shut off. Apparently, the Fragments had an issue with that and took it upon themselves to clog it up in its stead."

"Why would they?" Horace asked. "They're… Fragments. Why do that?"

Rumi shrugged, but Horace was already turning towards Aliyah. They'd mostly regained their elven shape now, as if the water clock's retrieval had calmed the compulsions transforming them.

"The Fragments are not mindless. I believe they are a reflection of where they live. This place has a history, and it affected them. They… I think they shared it with me, through the dreams. Beyond that… I am uncertain."

"All of its history?"

Keza's voice had dropped into a whisper, raw with longing. Her entire body leaned forward, ears perked as if it'd help catch Aliyah's every word.

"I am afraid not," they said. "It comes in, fittingly I suppose, fragments. Your people used to live in these mountains, did they not?"

"We think so, but all we have left is the village."

Aliyah tilted their head. "You owe me a story.

Would you share with me what you know of this one?"

A sharp laugh escaped Keza. "Not even gonna ask why I'm here to begin with? I suppose you're counting on Horace for that. E's just waiting to spill it all."

Horace snapped eir mouth shut. E'd been so ready to tell Aliyah everything they'd missed, but e'd promised not to, hadn't e? Keza had been very clear. "You've got to explain *some* things," e protested.

"I suppose, but not tonight."

She stretched, her motions exaggerated, and settled herself more. Part of Horace was disappointed she'd dodged the telling again, but exhaustion began to sink in. They'd spent hours in there, and the moon had crossed most of the sky by now.

"Rest first isn't too bad an idea," e said. "Don't you want a bed, Keza? That can't be comfortable."

Her tail curled around the wooden beam. "For you, perhaps. I wouldn't mind a hammock, but I've slept in worse than this. The height's nice."

Keza closed her eyes, and as far as Horace could tell, she was gone instantly. E turned to Rumi, eyebrows raised, but the little engineer shrugged. "I bet she just wants to impress."

"It's working." E couldn't sleep on a wooden beam like that! Even if eir quarters upstairs with Aliyah were tight, e at least had a solid mattress under em.

Rumi stifled a yawn, then patted eir leg. "Horace, friend, she fell from the sky and kicked your ass, and you'd have already given everything for five more minutes with her."

Had e been wrong, though? Even Rumi liked her, and now e had someone to teach em how to fight. They had a long way to travel still before they reached Alleaze, and Horace hoped that by the time they ran into trouble again, e'd be able to hold eir own better. For all of her sharp barbs, Keza had been nicer to em than any other mentor except Varena, and unlike most of them, she believed in em. For that alone, Horace would stand by her side no matter what Rumi or the Elders or anyone else thought of her.

It took Rumi a week to repair the clock, closed off in his workshop, in full work mode. Keza spent most of these either training Horace or scavenging for food in the mountains, once leaving them for so long she slept in the wilderness rather than returning to the Wagon. Horace suspected she avoided Aliyah and the owed story, but since Aliyah themself didn't press the issue when Keza was around, e held eir peace and pushed the limits of eir patience once again.

At least reinstalling the water hourglass required Horace's help. E heaved the cylinder back to the control room, Rumi fussing over eir every step as if he could prevent em from tripping. If anything, the additional stress made Horace more worried about it, but e ultimately reached their destination without incident and placed the cylinder down as instructed. E held it as Rumi secured it, and soon water coursed through it once again. They watched it fill the top half, then steadily drip down.

"There you go," Rumi declared. "With its brand-new counter, it'll be handling the water flow as seasons pass, saving up in rainier months for your dry spells."

Keza closed her eyes, tail curling around her leg as she inhaled slowly, then released. "Wish I could tell Elder Mawar who fixed it for them," she said, before turning towards Rumi. "Thank you, shortscales."

Rumi huffed. "Did it for Aliyah, not you."

Horace suspected he'd done it for the challenge as much as for anyone's sake, but e didn't call Rumi on his bluff.

"It is good, I think, to leave the places we travel through in a better state," Aliyah said. "Your help is appreciated."

It was the last any of them said on the subject, but Keza's mood remained strange all evening, hovering between nostalgic and broody, and as they settled around a dinner of rabbit slices and wild berry sauce, she finally told Aliyah what had happened while they recovered, deftly skirting any mention of her family. Aliyah listened with such intensity that they forgot their plate more often than not.

"So your people's secrecy," Aliyah said once Keza had finished, "it is historical?"

"Yes. And vital, according to the elders, though no one seems to know why anymore. Or they just wouldn't tell me. We should get going. Pass has dried out, hasn't it? And they don't want me around here."

The Wagon started with a soft creak, the gentle crush of its wheels on stone a familiar melody. They climbed to the top platform as they reached the Inari Pass again, watching the mossy patterns on the wall light up as the exit's sunlight grew more distant. Mud clung to the wheels as it rolled through the once-flooded area and continued forward, towards the other side of the Tesrima Ridge, and in time the coastal city of Alleaze. The thought of the ocean sent Horace's heart in a scramble of excitement and fear. It was the one thing every traveller promised was breathtaking. But that was a word e'd have used for the desert and mountains and secret valley village, too, so how incredible would the ocean be? Of this group, only Rumi had been there, and he'd answered Horace's questions with "you'll see."

In time, the Wagon emerged on the other side to a setting sun and an endless expanse of green treetops. Horace gaped at the forest, a sea onto itself, the trees gigantic despite the distance. The lush valley hadn't prepared em for this, and e stared at it for so long, unable to pull away, that when e did climb back down into the Wagon, dinner was ready and a game of Thorny Bush awaited em on the table.

"Oh! You could have fetched me," e said, a bit sheepish.

"We were about to," Rumi piped up. "Apparently, Keza is in *a sharing mood* and we all ought to be grateful for it."

From Keza's eye roll and the derisive way he'd said sharing mood, Horace guessed he was repeating Keza's own words. She tapped the table with her claw. "Just sit your ass and watch a master at work while I pay my story debt."

Horace complied, dragging a chair out for em to settle in, and placing the plate on eir lap. As e shoved the first bite of herb-dusted skewer in eir mouth, Keza leaned towards the pile of twigs and removed the first easy target.

One stick at a time, Keza unravelled the Thorny Bush, her attention focused on the diminishing pile of sticks as she began, slowly but surely, to paint a picture of the Tesrima Ridge's inhabitants. She spoke of a secret monastery in the mountain, most of its residents either dwarves or felnexi, and of a thriving community centred around traditions lost to time; spoke of sacred flowers and a fighting style that was said to encompass the tale of the world and was now used to push Fragments away. What happened to them, she could not say. Her tone stayed irreverent, but a sense of loss permeated her words—for everything they'd forgotten, and everything she was leaving behind. In time, Keza picked up the second-to-last stick, and only a twisting twig remained at the middle of the table. She twirled one of her conquered sticks nonchalantly.

"So that's the story of the Inae Tradition, or what crumbs we know of it and protect. Whatever pushed them to secrecy centuries ago was such that it became a primordial tenet, and is almost all that survived—alongside the Inae Dance." She picked up the last stick and locked gaze with Aliyah. "Did you see them, in your dreams? My ancestors?"

"I believe so, yes." They closed their eyes, as if to better remember. "Dwarves supervising the canals, felnexi exchanging blue flowers in a ceremony, children of all races leaping into a swirling, steaming pool. Little moments of joy and life, but some of panic too. The mountain shaking, roaring water in the distance, screams through the tunnel. Flashes of golden light. I do not know what happened to them, however, but perhaps secrecy was warranted."

"That's horrible," Horace said, halfway to another bath. "You think the Fragments did this? That golden light?"

"Conceivably," Aliyah offered, "but the dreams are always confusing. I cannot know for sure."

"Regardless, it's not my tale, not anymore," Keza said, a tightness to her voice betraying her dismissiveness. She pressed on, though, clearly determined to change subject. "It seems to me you have your own unique thing going on. So tell me where this merry band is headed for, and one day that might be my tale, too."

Keza didn't need to add "if you'll have me". It went unstated, and not even Rumi raised a protest. She'd dropped into their lives like a hurricane, full of secrets and snark, but Horace couldn't imagine her splitting now. Even if she never spoke of home again, e wanted her to have someone who'd seen it and understood what she'd lost. And maybe, given enough time, she'd think of the Wagon as home, too, in its own way.

THE STORY CONTINUES....

The Wagon's crew has reached Alleaze, a coastal city from which they hope to book passage across the ocean. But Alleaze's regular life has stopped, giving way to the excitement of the Sea Spirit Festival, a weeks-long event filled with games and seafood delicacies. What pleasure the crew gets from the festivities is cut short when the event's crowning moment—the choosing of a Storm Catcher by the Bay's Spirit—never unfolds. In order to help Alleaze find its local hero and be allowed to sail out, they will need to confront the truth behind the legend of the Sea Spirit—and survive it.

Excerpt from THE SEA SPIRIT FESTIVAL

When Trenaze held festivities, it took over the Grand Market for a few days, providing a central location for all residents to gather.

Alleaze, it seemed, celebrated throughout the city as a whole.

Every street was covered in decorations— some with colourful bunting flags marked with symbols, others with flower garlands, or large nets had been dangled between balconies, or even strings of fish bones and sea shells glued together and painted over. Alleazans would have stalls right outside their doors, selling food and jewelry and clothes, or they'd stroll through the crowds with the wares attached to their body, hanging from their shoulders and on a small table. Everywhere Horace turned, people traded with tokens, chattering and laughing.

Pockets of the city *had* been dedicated to specific endeavours, though. A large portion of the docks held a gigantic fish market, with fresh catches and large specimens marked as "blessed by the Sea Spirit"—which, locals told Horace, meant they'd never spoil, and had often been caught months or even years ago. Sellers would label their age on little seashells or wooden placards, and these racked up far more tokens than regular fish. Across from this market was one full of nets, fishing poles, cages, lures, and a wide variety of tools Horace had never seen in eir life. When Horace started stopping at every table to muddle through explanations, struggling with the accents in the ambient noise,

Rumi grabbed eir hand and pulled em away.

"Satisfy your curiosity later. Jameela mentioned games, and those are where we can win more tokens."

Even though e knew they had up to an entire month in the city, e pouted. What if e forgot to come back?

"I want to know, too," Aliyah said. "We can return together."

That was enough for Horace. Aliyah had a much better memory than em. It was so good, Horace sometimes thought they absorbed information and never let it go.

In time, they found an old public square transformed to hold a host of games. Their first clue of its location came from jolly music and loud bells, tailed by laughter and excited cheering. Then the crowd thickened, the steady stream turning into a slow morass of people. Keza slunk closer to em, always on eir heels, and e was careful not to push between groups where she couldn't follow.

Eir mindfulness disintegrated when they reached the square proper, and all the options extended before em. Horace towered over a great deal of the crowd, and e had no trouble sweeping eir gaze across the grounds, absorbing the countless opportunities offered to them: a cluster of grills and cooking apparatus from which drifted a delicious scent—to snack between games, e figured—a plethora of stalls with challenges of luck or address, two very big vats filled with water with an obscure purpose, and tables with individual games and trinkets that, at a distance, reminded em of Rumi's work.

Horace's mind was spinning with the possibilities, and e couldn't decide where to start when a powerful voice boomed across the fairgrounds, burying the noise of the crowd.

"Do *you* have what it takes to be the Storm Catcher? Come, come, gather here and test your strength!"

Horace had no idea what a storm catcher was, but e had a fair amount of muscles and even more curiosity. E stretched on eir tiptoes, scanning in the general direction of the voice until e spotted a black-furred munonoxi with bulging biceps and tiny, clearly shaved off horns. The pronoun pin—green for he/him—had been tied to the horns, in bold display.

"Only two tokens to try!" the munonoxi called. "Come on now, don't be shy!"

"Rumi," Horace started.

Before Horace could ask, eir friend had slapped two of the tokens in eir hand. "You show this town, Horace."

Continue the journey!

books2read.com/seaspiritfestival-nerezia

NEVER MISS AN UPDATE

www.claudiearseneault.com/newsletter

About the Author

Claudie Arseneault is an easily-enthused aromantic and asexual writer with a never-ending cycle of obsessions but an enduring love for all things cephalopod and fantasy (together or not!). She writes stories that centre platonic relationships and loves large casts and single-city settings, the most notable of which are the City of Spires series (2017-2023) and Baker Thief (2018).

In addition to her own fiction, Claudie has co-edited Common Bonds (2021), an anthology of aromantic speculative short stories. She is a founding member of The Kraken Collective, an alliance of self-publishing SFF authors, and the creator of the Aromantic and Asexual Characters Database.

Find out more at claudiearseneault.com

Other Great Books From The Kraken Collective!

Fancy another short read? The Kraken Collective has plenty of shorter works to offer! From cozy sci-fi short stories to sapphic romance, you're sure to find something to read.

krakencollectivebooks.com

Acknowledgements

One of the hardest part of acknowledgements, I find, is knowing where to start—who to start with. There are so many to name, isn't there?

But there are people out there, people whose name I often don't know, who made this book possible by making me want to keep going. And that's all the readers who go seeking out queer stories that don't center romance, all the readers who don't see aromantic and asexual characters as afterthoughts, who don't think of queerness as F/F, M/M, Trans, and the Others, the "pairing not applicable". When you write stories like mine, navigating the queer book community is a fraught endeavour, a space filled the caltrops of exclusion and dismissiveness, a thousand small cuts. So all those readers who take time for us, who give the platonic queer stories, the no romance adventures and what-else-have-you the love and attention they deserve? Those readers mean the world to me, and they have, without a doubt, made Nerezia and all of my books possible. I do not know that I would have had the stamina to keep going without them. So thank you, truly, from the bottom of my heart.

As for the production of this book, well, many of the aforementioned readers are no doubt part of my amazing Kickstarter backers, who through their contributions have pushed us all the way to the *Flooded Secrets* stretch goal, covering most of its costs.

Those funds went into some incredibly talented people: my cover artist, Eva, who continues to bring to life my universe in one long canvas; my line artist, Vanessa, and my super editor, Lynn. Special thanks, also, to Cedar and Quartzen, who through reading and brainstorming continue to help bring these stories to bright, vibrant life.

I also have a great support social circle — friends of the Kraken Collective, fellow writers in discords and on social media, my partner, who keeps believing in me, my mom, who will line her most prized shelves with my books. Thank you all for the love.